HER LAST STEPS

A PSYCHOLOGICAL SUSPENSE THRILLER

N. L. HINKENS

This is a work of fiction. Names, characters, organizations, places, events and incidents are either products of the author's imagination or are used fictitiously. For more information about the author, please visit www.normahinkens.com

Published by Dunecadia Publishing, California

ISBN: 978-1-947890-17-6

Cover by: www.derangeddoctordesign.com

Editing by: www.jeanette-morris.com/first-impressions-writing

❀ Created with Vellum

PROLOGUE

"*Can I run, Mommy?*"

Ava Galbraith flinched and pressed her knuckles to her lips. Her daughter's last words ricocheted around inside her skull like metal balls, echoed by the sound of her tiny footsteps crunching the icy surface beneath her like the dry Cheerios she'd eaten for breakfast that morning. Footsteps Ava might never hear again. Dread, more numbing than the frigid air chilling her cheeks, shot through her, trailed by the forlorn bleat of an animal in pain. She blinked at the snowy expanse that stretched for miles in every direction before it dawned on her that the desolate cry had come from her own lips. She shouldn't have returned. She should have run and never looked back.

One last, long weekend to tie up all the loose ends, she'd promised herself. And to pick up the collateral she would need to take him down. Ava and her four-year-old daughter, Melanie, had arrived late Wednesday afternoon and set out early the next morning to take pictures of the wraithlike lake at dawn. A heavy storm was forecast for that evening, and Ava was eager to capture what she could of the area before it hit, especially the spectacular peaks which rose like a frosted granite stockade around the lake. She was closing in on one-hundred-thousand followers on her Instagram and making decent money from the sponsored posts she featured—a stream of income she sorely needed thanks to Gordon's sporadic child support payments. At least that's what she told herself. It was easier than admitting to what she had set in motion. She had covered her tracks well, rehearsed her narrative until she almost believed it, but the fear of everything unraveling fermented inside her.

Shortly before seven, she woke her daughter and, after packing up a quick breakfast of cereal in a baggie for Melanie and hot coffee in a thermos for her, they pulled on their coats, hats, gloves, and boots, and headed down the trail toward the lake, a solid mass shrouded in a dove-gray dawn. Their frozen breath dangled in front of them as they trudged along, hand-in-hand, the black rocks that scattered the shoreline frosted with a light dusting of snow. The lake groaned and grated—testing its icy bonds, unable to resist the call of spring. In a few short months, it would be brimming with birdsong and dragonflies, the laughter of children doing backflips off rickety docks, and the gentle plopping sounds of fishermen casting their lines. Ava and Melanie wouldn't be here to witness it of course, but that was all part of the plan.

"It's twinkling, Mommy!" Melanie clapped her hands and squealed with the pure delight of a four-year-old as she scooped up a palmful of snow in her purple mittens. Ava smiled and marveled with her as she took several shots of her daughter in quick succession trying to capture her expression of wonder. Her creamy skin was flushed against the biting morning air, framed by dark chestnut curls tumbling out from under her woolen cap with the ridiculously oversized glitter yarn pom-pom she'd insisted Gammy —as she called Gordon's mother—make for it. Ava felt a familiar sickening twist in her stomach at the thought of her mother-in-law. Patricia Galbraith with her smoky brows, slick silver bob, and tongue as razor-edged as her jaw, had gone all out to press her thin lips together in a cold smile when they'd first met. Their relationship since that first arctic encounter hadn't progressed beyond tepid. Patricia had only tolerated her as long as she served her purpose as a socially suitable and dutiful wife to Gordon. They hadn't spoken at all since Ava and Gordon separated last Christmas. If things went as planned, they would never speak again.

Ava collected her rambling thoughts and knelt for a moment by a rock to take a photograph of the ski runs crisscrossing the mountains like silver scars on the other side of the lake. She looked through the viewfinder and locked the center focus point, sucking in a hard breath at the staggering beauty of the snow-filled veins traversing the mountains. The play of light and shadow on the frosty expanse surrounding the lake lent an element of drama to the surreal scene. It was the perfect shot that blurred the lines between art and life, fact and fiction. Ava had gotten particularly good at blurring those lines of late. Gordon thought her incapable of subterfuge, and she had no intention of correcting his misconception until it was too late for him to do anything about it.

When she turned back around, Melanie had disappeared from view. "Wait for Mommy, Mels!" Ava called out gaily.

When her daughter didn't respond, she hastily packed away her lens and scrambled to her feet, tamping down a niggling worry before setting out to catch up with her. But, several minutes later, Melanie was still nowhere to be seen. As best Ava could make out, her daughter's footprints led away from the lake toward the road, like faint, silver shadows in the hard-packed snow, and then simply vanished. It made no sense. Ava frowned, trying to compute where her daughter could be. A ball of lava-like fear smoldered in her chest as she agonized over what could possibly have happened. How long had she spent taking pictures? She'd lost all track of time, something she tended to do when engrossed in her work. Five, six minutes, longer? Long enough for a four-year-old to run into trouble. But surely not long enough to climb the steep embankment to the road? Ava's pulse thudded as her fear mounted. Melanie's foot-prints indicated she hadn't made it as far as the road, but the ground was so frozen it was difficult to be sure a lightweight like her daughter would leave much of an imprint.

Ava darted frantic glances in every direction before

hurriedly retracing her steps, repeatedly calling out her daughter's name. Her heart shuddered beneath her ribs like a train changing tracks. Tracks that, moments earlier, had been taking her on a weekend full of the promise of newfound freedom and a fresh start, were suddenly taking her against her will into a dark tunnel of indeterminate length. The kind of house of horror train ride you heard about on the evening news that took parents to lonely, desolate places they didn't want to believe could exist. A hideous nightmare that shouldn't be happening to her. She was a good mother, wasn't she? She had made plans to save them from the danger they were in—the danger Gordon had put them in. And now this...

Squeezing her eyes shut against the blinding brightness of the snow, she forced herself to think rationally. Maybe she'd missed something. Melanie had to be close by. She was only four—how far could a four-year-old walk in a couple of minutes? *But Melanie had been running!* Ava gasped. Her daughter could be farther away than she'd imagined, or she might have tripped and become buried in the snow. Fighting her rising panic, Ava began hunting methodically around the area, digging with the fervor of a dog unearthing a bone, yelling for her daughter until her throat was raw. She walked in increasingly hopeless circles, widening her search, but there was no way to tell which direction Melanie had gone.

A quick glance at the deserted lake confirmed she hadn't wandered out on the frozen surface. It would be weeks before the ice began to break apart anyway—ruling out the possibility that she'd drowned.

Think, Ava, think!

There must be a less macabre explanation. Melanie was in all likelihood playing in a snowdrift somewhere, her thick woolen hat muffling the sound of her mother's frantic cries. Ava cast another desperate glance around at the endless white carpet rolled out as far as the eye could see in every direction, and then set out at a determined pace along the perimeter of the lake. Her camera bag slapped haphazardly on her hip as she scoured the area for any sign that her daughter had continued their walk around the lake without her. As she drew in jagged breaths, she racked her brains for a rational explanation of why Melanie's footsteps abruptly stopped. Had someone picked her up and carried her off? Ava's breath caught in her throat and she quickened her pace. She hadn't noticed a third set of footprints—only hers and Melanie's.

Another hideous thought soon wormed its way into her distraught mind. What if a wild animal had carried Melanie away? Like the dingo story in Australia. Or even a bear, perhaps? She forced air into her lungs, chiding herself for needless fearmongering. The only wolves in the entire state roamed the wilderness hundreds of miles north, and everyone knew that bears hibernated in winter. The only creature they were likely to encounter in the early hours at the lake was a harmless deer or a curious fox. She stifled a groan. That wasn't necessarily a good thing either. Melanie was fascinated by foxes. If she'd spotted one, she might have followed it. Only yesterday, they'd seen one hanging around outside the cabin, its bushy tail curled beneath it, watching the door, as if testing the extent of their hospitality. At Melanie's insistence, they'd set an egg out on the back porch and watched as the hungry creature surreptitiously snuck it off the deck and loped off between the trees to enjoy its loot.

Ava retraced her steps and studied the area where her daughter's footprints disappeared more closely. The snow was flattened in parts, which was curious, but there were no clear tracks leading away from the location. Thankfully, there was no evidence of blood, or signs of a scuffle, which gave her some small measure of comfort that nothing heinous had transpired. She shivered at the dire scenarios her thoughts so quickly gravitated toward; feral animals, and wild-eyed serial killers topping the list. But, this was sleepy Brooksbury, the safest community on the planet. Gordon had grown up here, and they'd been coming to the lake as a family for years. Bad things didn't happen here.

As the minutes went by, Ava's search grew more and more frenzied, her every rational thought melding in a torrent of panic. She kicked at banks of snow, screaming out Melanie's name over and over, listening to it reverberate around the empty lake, desperately trying to keep alive a smidgen of hope that at some point her daughter would peek out from behind a pile of snow, her laugh tinkling through the crisp, morning air as she yelled, "Your turn to hide, Mommy!"

Salty tears pricked at Ava's eyes. She shot a glance toward the distant spires of smoke rising up from the few, remote cabins nestled in the foothills on the other side of the lake. She couldn't rule out the possibility that someone had taken Melanie. But the idea sounded even more ridiculous than the notion that a wild animal had run off with her daughter in its jaws. Ava chewed on her lip contemplating another disturbing thought. What about a drifter? Or a hitchhiker passing through? It seemed unlikely. The harsh conditions didn't make Brooksbury an appealing stop for anyone sleeping rough. As she rapidly eliminated every possibility that sprang to mind, her head began to pound with a new fear. Could this be connected to what she'd uncovered? But, how did they know she was here?

She shivered, darting another glance around, all at once unsure of who or what she was looking for, wondering if her well-laid plans had come together too late to save her and Melanie. A gentle snowfall was already alighting on the trees around her. She estimated she'd been searching for her daughter for close to an hour. If her worst fears were realized, Melanie was in extreme danger from the kind of people who had no qualms about doing whatever it took to protect their secrets. Ava scratched frantically at her scalp. She should seek help before the day was spent and the storm rolled in. The tumult in her head grew louder as she weighed the risks of involving the police in an investigation which might turn up more than she wanted it to. Should she call Gordon first? Probably not a good idea. If she gave him control, she couldn't be sure he would put their daughters's safety first—not with everything that was at stake. After a moment's hesitation, she turned and ran back toward the log cabin that had been in her husband's family for three generations. She'd forgotten to charge her phone last night which left her with no choice but to drive all the way into town to alert the sheriff. Time was racing away from her, and with it any hope of assembling a search party and finding Melanie before darkness fell.

Heaving for breath as the cabin came into sight, Ava flung open the door of her station wagon parked in the driveway, jumped inside and revved the engine before tearing off down the narrow, rutted lane. As she veered out onto the main road, hot waves of terror washed over her at the thought of leaving Melanie alone in the white silence of the brooding lake. But, if someone had taken her daughter, she would never find her without help. The sooner she alerted the authorities, the better. Everyone knew the first forty-eight hours were the most critical.

Two miles down the road, Patricia Galbraith's house came into view, a lavish rustic retreat of natural stone and cedar that Gordon had built for her when he and Ava got married. The curtains were tightly drawn and the house was in darkness, but Ava slammed on the brakes regardless. Gordon's mother was in Chicago on a shopping trip with a girlfriend—which was one of the reasons Ava had chosen this weekend to come up to the cabin to wrap things up. It was highly unlikely Melanie had wandered this far on her own, but it would only take a moment to check. She jumped out, leaving the engine running, and hammered on the front door. "Patricia! Anyone home?" After scouring the front and back yard for any sign of Melanie, Ava ran back to her car and rammed it into gear.

As she swerved out onto the main road again, sweat beaded on her forehead, despite the brisk temperature inside her vehicle. No doubt the sheriff would deploy a search party right away. Soon, everyone in Brooksbury would know Melanie was missing—that she had failed as a mother. This was supposed to have been her final stay at the lake, a bittersweet farewell of sorts. Not just to the cabin, but to everything it represented; her intact family, all the memories yet to be made that had dissolved along with the countless tears she had shed over the dark secrets she had stumbled across.

She'd planned on breaking the news of her and Gordon's impending divorce to mutual friends and neighbors this weekend. Now, she faced a far more dreadful proposition.

2

*D*etective Mallory Anderson fixed a keen gaze on Gordon Galbraith's distraught wife who sat crumpled in the chair opposite him in the small sheriff station on the edge of Brooksbury. Limp, blonde hair framed her pale, oval face like a shroud, magnifying swollen, violet eyes that stared vacantly past him, looking as lost as her missing daughter. Either the woman was genuinely gutted, or she deserved an Academy award for the heart-wrenching performance she had just given. He had little reason to doubt her somewhat puzzling story of her missing four-year-old daughter as she'd recounted it, but he would make every effort to verify it before he began an official investigation that would require dispatching Search and Rescue in the looming blizzard.

Eying the camera she fiddled with constantly in her lap, he recalled that Ava Galbraith was an avid photographer, and an exceptionally good one. He'd even bought a set of her framed photographs of the lake at the annual craft fair two summers ago and hung them up in the family room. To his annoyance, his wife, Tammy replaced them soon after with some cheap prints she picked up at a chain discount store which he was less than enamored with. He'd learned to keep his mouth shut though. Things were prickly enough between the two of them without starting a pointless argument over home decor that might well escalate into another cold war of indeterminate length and chill factor. They couldn't go on like this much longer. His heart felt like a shriveled piece of fruit in his chest that had long since decomposed. Despite the efforts he'd made to prop up their marriage, it was becoming increasingly obvious that Tammy had no interest in trying to rekindle what they'd once shared.

"Do you have a photo of Melanie?" Mallory gestured to Ava's camera.

When she didn't respond, he added in a low, composed tone. "Mrs. Galbraith, did you happen to take a picture of your daughter at the lake this morning? Before she went missing?"

Ava blinked uncertainly and then her eyes widened in understanding. "Oh, yes, of course! You need to know what she was wearing." She hastily pulled the nylon camera strap over her head and began clicking through the pictures before passing the camera to Mallory. He studied the screen, schooling his expression to neutral as he took in the gap-toothed smile of the chocolate-eyed child beneath the knit purple hat with the glitter pom-pom that was almost as big as the head it adorned. She was Gordon's double, a Galbraith through and through. The smile was trusting, believing, a smile of faith in the mother behind the lens—misplaced faith as it turned out. Rotten luck to have scored two loser parents. A pang of conscience hit as he inwardly acknowledged it might be an unfair judgement of Ava Galbraith. He didn't know her particularly well, unlike her overbearing husband. Although he didn't have kids of his own, Mallory harbored a low tolerance for people who neglected or abused their offspring. Losing a four-year-old next to a frozen lake fell into that category in his black-and-white world.

He glanced up from the camera. "What about pictures of the area where her footprints petered out—you mentioned the ground nearby had been flattened?"

Ava stared back at him, a look of horror forming on her pale face. "I never even thought about taking a picture of it." She dropped her head into her hands and let out a reproachful groan. "I'm such an idiot! I was so focused on searching for Melanie. It never occurred to me to document anything."

"That's understandable," Mallory soothed, trying to curb the irritation in his voice. Seemed to him like the logical thing for a photographer to do in the circumstances, but then again Ava hadn't been thinking straight as she'd admitted. The way she described it, she'd panicked and basically run around in circles until she'd made the decision to seek help. Mallory cast an appraising glance out the window at the snow beginning to come down outside. Too bad she hadn't thought to put her camera to good use—any remaining tracks would be completely covered up with fresh powder by the time a search party got out there now.

Motioning to his junior partner, Brent, seated at a desk jammed in the corner of the cramped office, Mallory held out Ava's camera to him. "Get Melanie's picture printed up right away. We'll need copies for the file, and Search and Rescue, and make up some missing person's flyers while you're at it."

Brent nodded, shooting Ava a pitying look before disappearing down the hallway with the camera.

Mallory turned his attention back to Ava who was intermittently picking at the skin around her nails now that her camera was no longer at her disposal.

"Does Melanie have any medical conditions that we

should be aware of?" he asked, reaching for a pen from the plastic tray on his desk.

Ava gave an aggravated shake of her head. "No! She's perfectly healthy. But she won't be for much longer if we don't find her soon. Can't you get Search and Rescue out there to start looking for her?" She tossed a harried glance over her shoulder at the snow accumulating on the window ledge outside the station. "I should drive back. I need to be there in case she finds her way back to the cabin."

"We're working on getting a search and rescue crew together," Mallory assured her. "Give us a few more minutes. I have an officer on the phone checking urgent care, and doctor's offices, in case someone picked Melanie up wandering along the road. Are you certain you didn't hear a snowmobile or a car engine start up anywhere in the vicinity? Or voices?"

A look of annoyance flickered in Ava's eyes. "Like I told you already, Melanie and I were the only ones out there. It was too early for dog walkers. Why are you asking me the same questions over and over again instead of doing something constructive to find my daughter? If someone had driven off with her, don't you think I would have heard them?" She threw up her hands in frustration. "There weren't any vehicles—"

"Mrs. Galbraith—"

"It's *Miss*!" Ava snapped. "At least it will be soon enough. I'm reverting to my maiden name, Marsh." Her shoulders sagged and she went on in a defeated tone, "Just call me Ava. You know my soon-to-be ex well enough to drop the formalities, sheriff."

Mallory hefted a brow at the news. He formed a suitably sympathetic smile on his lips while making a careful note of the information. He shared more history than he cared to admit to with Gordon Galbraith. None of which he looked back on fondly. The man had always been a pompous jerk, as far back as high school. Still, it seemed a stretch to think he could have had anything to do with his daughter's disappearance from the lake. There were easier ways for him to make off with her if it came to that. Nonetheless, if little Melanie Galbraith hadn't simply wandered off on her own and got lost in the snow somewhere, her parents' looming divorce would be a line of inquiry he would be pursuing. It was no secret that most abducted children ended up being taken by their own parents, especially if an acrimonious split was in the mix. Mallory twisted his pen between his fingers. Even if it turned out that her father had taken her, it didn't mean Melanie was safe. Feuding parents had been known to do terrible things to their own children to ensure their estranged partners didn't get custody. He grimaced. "Rest assured, Mrs—*Ava*, We're doing everything in our power to find Melanie as quickly as possible. I just need to ask you a few more questions while we're waiting on Search and Rescue."

Ava let out an exasperated sigh and looked away, her eyes glassy with tears.

Mallory pretended to study his notes before clearing his throat and continuing, "Do you and Gordon both have legal custody of Melanie?"

Ava clenched her fists on the desk in front of her. "Yes, we still have to work all that out—you know, the terms of the divorce, visitation, dividing up the assets and so on. Gordon wants to keep the cabin of course, it's been in his family forever. That's part of the reason I came up here this weekend, to clear out my things. I didn't tell anyone I was coming, I wanted to keep it on the QT. This was to have been our—my last trip to the lake."

Mallory didn't miss the slip she'd hastened to correct. Evidently, Ava was bent on getting full custody of her daughter and had no intention of letting Melanie come back to Brooksbury with her father. It struck Mallory as odd that Ava felt compelled to explain to him what she was doing at the cabin. Was she hiding something? From him, or from Gordon? Instead of pressing the issue, he gave an understanding nod as he scribbled down his observations and underlined *potential custody battle* on his notepad. "Does Gordon know you brought Melanie up to the cabin this weekend?"

"Of course! I had to tell him." Ava huffed in annoyance. "He's her father."

"How did he react?"

Ava shrugged. "He was livid that I picked a weekend when his mother was gone. He accused me of trying to keep Melanie from seeing her grandmother. Aside from that, I don't think he cared one way or another. He just wanted my stuff out."

Mallory furrowed his brow. "I'm sorry to have to ask you such a delicate question, but are you and Gordon currently living together?"

Ava's cheeks flushed. "In a manner of speaking. When we separated at Christmas, he moved into the adjoining guest house on our property in Cedarville. This weekend was supposed to have been a welcome break for me from our current living situation. It's hard to ignore someone who still pulls in and out of your driveway every day." She managed a rueful grin. "Petty, I know. I'm sure you can't relate."

Mallory dropped his gaze and made a show of jotting down the information. If only she knew just how much he empathized with her situation. He'd signed up to go on a ridiculously overpriced fly fishing trip with his cousin next month for that very reason—*a welcome reprieve*. He had no particular affection for fishing, or his beer-guzzling, younger cousin, but the thought of being away from

Tammy and the stifling atmosphere at home for three straight days had been too enticing to pass up. He understood exactly why Ava Galbraith was willing to drive five hours to get away from a moldering marriage, if only for a few days.

"Is Gordon in Cedarville this weekend?" Mallory continued.

Ava twisted her lips. "As far as anyone knows."

Mallory sensed resentment in her voice. Surely since they shared a daughter together, they needed to keep each other in the loop on their schedules. But, Gordon Galbraith might not be cooperating when it came to sharing those kinds of details. Or he may have intentionally misled her. Before Mallory had a chance to press Ava on the issue, Brent stuck his head around the edge of the door. "Search and Rescue are on their way to the address with tracking dogs."

"Tell them we'll meet them there." Mallory replaced the cap on his pen, pocketed his notebook and nodded to Ava as he stood. "You can ride with me in the squad car in case any leads come in en route and we need to make a detour. I'll have Brent drive your vehicle back to your cabin."

Ava climbed into the back seat of the squad car and plugged in her seat belt as Mallory backed out of the station parking lot.

"What if Melanie's been abducted by a stranger?" Ava asked, leaning back on the seat and staring straight ahead. "What if we're wasting our time searching for her at the lake?"

"It's unlikely. Not many strangers around these parts. But we'll cover every angle," Mallory replied in as reassuring a tone as he could muster. "We've put out a be-on-the-lookout alert with Melanie's description, and set up a road block on the main highway leaving town. If an abductor attempts to flee the area, he won't get far."

Of course, there was always the sobering possibility that an abductor might have already fled the area, but Mallory kept that observation to himself, instead shooting Ava a questioning look in the rearview mirror. "I take it you didn't search your cabin before you drove to the station?"

Ava frowned and shook her head slowly. "I … I wasn't thinking straight—"

"It's all right," Mallory interrupted. "Not trying to send you on another guilt trip. Just wanted to make sure we know where to start looking before we dispatch SAR. You'd be surprised how often a missing child turns up at home. If Melanie got lost and found her way back to the cabin, she might curl up somewhere to sleep, or hide in a closet or someplace similar if she was frightened."

Ava let out a little whimper. "Maybe I should have stayed at the lake."

"No. You did the right thing notifying us immediately so we could initiate SAR before the weather worsens," Mallory affirmed, drumming his fingers on the steering wheel as he drove. "What about Gordon's mother, Patricia Galbraith? Doesn't she live close by? Any chance Melanie could have walked to her house?"

Ava turned to stare out the window. "She's not here this weekend. She's in Chicago. I took a quick look around the outside of the property before I drove into town. There was no sign of Melanie, or footprints, or anything else to indicate she'd been there."

"Do you have a key to Patricia's place?"

"No. I … I haven't talked to my mother-in-law since Gordon told her we're getting divorced."

Mallory wasn't surprised to hear that Ava's relationship with her mother-in-law wasn't a close one. Patricia

Galbraith's air of superiority rubbed most people the wrong way. Tammy couldn't stand the woman either, but then she'd had numerous run-ins with her all the way back to high school. Gordon's mother had always turned up her nose at anyone from the trailer park where Tammy grew up, and the fact that Tammy's father was a convicted felon was the final affront to Patricia's social sensibilities.

"What about your parents?" Mallory inquired. "Do they live nearby?"

"They died in a car crash when I was eight-years-old," Ava answered. "My Aunt Delia raised me, she lives in Cedarville. I ... haven't called her yet to let her know that Melanie's missing."

"What about Gordon? Have you told him?"

"No." Ava sniffed. After a dead weight pause, she added, "He'll use it against me in court. He's determined to get custody of Melanie." She shot Mallory a pleading look in the mirror. "Search and Rescue might find her soon. I'm hoping I won't have to make that call."

Mallory kept his concentration fixed on the road. He wasn't going to lie to her. If they didn't find the kid at the cabin, Ava would have to inform Gordon, or he would be forced to make the call for her. He didn't blame her for wanting to avoid a confrontation with her husband. Mallory had been on the receiving end of Gordon's rage a time or two himself. The worst was the night of their senior prom when Gordon smashed the windscreen of his car so Mallory couldn't drive Tammy home.

Tammy and Gordon had dated for a few months in high school, but that was before Mallory had swept her off her feet. At least that's how she'd described it back then. At six-foot-four he had a good six inches on Gordon Galbraith, and with a footballer's build, strong jaw, and a thick head of wavy hair, he'd never had any problem attracting female attention.

Gordon, on the other hand, was already bald at thirty-seven and never quite managed to fill out those expensive suits of his in all the right places. Still, Mallory couldn't help wondering if Gordon's extraordinary success in business might outweigh his own assets if Tammy had the chance to do it all over.

3

*W*hen Mallory turned down the potholed lane to the cabin, Ava passed a shaking hand over her forehead at the sight of all the vehicles parked haphazardly on the grounds of her property, a motley collection of heavy-duty trucks, four-wheel drive jeeps and squad cars. Two men were busy unloading a utility snowmobile and portable floodlights from the bed of a truck. Ava's heart convulsed in her chest. How long did they think it was going to take to find Melanie? A four-year-old would never survive out here at night in freezing temperatures.

Ava blinked around in growing horror. Her worst fears had been realized. This was no nightmare from which she would awaken momentarily. This was actually happening. Melanie, her beautiful, precious daughter was missing, an official incident on Sheriff Mallory's roster, a *have-you-seen-me* cherub face on a throwaway flyer about to be handed out to random strangers. A cherub face Ava might have kissed for the last time this morning. Bile surged up her throat and she swallowed hard to contain her terror as Mallory rolled to a stop and parked behind a large black truck.

He turned around in the seat and looked pointedly at her. "Doing all right?" His hooded, blue eyes searched hers, pooling with compassion. He gave a chagrined shake of his head. "Sorry, that was a dumb question. I know you're not all right, but do you think you can do this?"

Ava responded with an uncertain nod. "What do I need to do?"

"For now, just make yourself available to answer any questions the police or the SAR team might have," Mallory explained. "With your permission, we'll begin by searching the cabin in case Melanie has returned in the meantime of her own accord. Like I said, it's not unusual to find scared kids hiding out in their own homes, hours, sometimes days, after they disappeared."

"Okay," Ava said weakly as she fumbled for a tissue to blow her nose. Her head throbbed, a new fear compounding inside her as she tried to assure herself that the officers wouldn't find what was hidden in the cabin. It wasn't like they'd be slitting cushions and tearing up floorboards. Regardless, she had little choice but to let them do their thing, and hope for the best. Searching the cabin for Melanie was just another frustrating hoop that had to be jumped through—Mallory couldn't exactly circumvent procedure. His constant reassurances gave her a sliver of hope that he would find her daughter eventually. But, would it be too late? She couldn't help thinking that Melanie's disappearance had everything to do with why she was leaving Gordon in the first place. And if she was right, Mallory and his team of experts were looking in all the wrong places.

The distant wail of a fire engine cut through the morning air, a keening sound that unleashed a fresh wave of terror in Ava's heart. She climbed out of the squad car on legs that threatened to fold and followed Mallory into the cabin where they were joined by his partner, Brent, and two more officers, their expressions schooled to neutral as they acknowledged her with solemn tilts of their heads.

"Are there any hidden crawl spaces in the house we should know about, other than the attic, or any places on the property where Melanie typically likes to hide?" Mallory asked her.

Ava shifted beneath his eagle-eyed gaze reminding herself again that the secrets the cabin held were safe for now, too well-concealed to be uncovered in a cursory search.

"Just the closets," Ava said. "I can check the—"

Mallory laid a firm hand on her arm, a quiet command in his voice. "I'm going to need you to take a seat and wait here while we conduct our search. We can't run the risk of contaminating any evidence we uncover."

Ava frowned, wondering what he was alluding to, but sank obediently down on the couch. What evidence was there to contaminate? Melanie had disappeared at the lake, not at the cabin. The only evidence had been her tiny footprints which now lay buried under a flurry of snow. Ava's heart clattered, echoing inside her ribcage when it dawned on her what Mallory was getting at. They couldn't allow her to help them look for her own child because they suspected she might be involved in her disappearance. Ava dropped her face into her shaking hands as the officers moved off to conduct their search. How had it come to this after everything she'd done to protect her daughter? One finite moment now forever divided her life into before and after. If something had happened to Melanie, there would be no end to this searing pain inside her, it would continue to burn throughout the years as birthdays came and went, and holidays blended together in an empty nod to what might have been. All her meticulous plans for their future as utterly undone as her heart.

She jerked her head up when Mallory strode back into

the room. She could tell at once that something had changed in his expression. A subtle foreboding in the set of his jaw told her it wasn't good news. She stood, fighting a wave of nausea as the room tilted and swayed around her, her mouth too dry to form the question that came to mind. She knew in her heart they hadn't found Melanie in the cabin, so what exactly had they discovered?

Mallory's eyes drilled into her as if waiting on her to speak first. Her throat tightened. It would be difficult to explain it away if they had found it. And they might have. The police were professionals after all. Despite Googling what she'd done repeatedly, she still wasn't sure if she'd committed a misdemeanor or a felony. She could be implicated in everything she'd uncovered about Gordon, maybe even accused of abducting her own daughter. Melanie's disappearance had interrupted the narrative she had worked so hard to perfect over the past few months. Everything was suddenly imploding around her. But maybe it didn't matter anymore. A life free from Gordon held no appeal without her daughter.

After what seemed like an eternal pause, Mallory cleared his throat. "One of my officers found traces of blood in the master bathroom. Any idea where it might have come from?"

Relief and confusion melded as one in Ava's brain. They hadn't found it. She stared at Mallory for a moment, her thoughts rocketing in myriad directions before she collected herself enough to respond, "Melanie had a nose bleed this morning." She gave a rueful grin and shrugged. "It's the altitude, she often gets them when we come up here."

Mallory's piercing eyes didn't leave Ava's face. "All right. We'll have forensics check it out."

"You don't believe me, do you?" Her voice wavered despite her indignation. Of course he suspected the blood spoke to something more ominous than a nosebleed. He was wasting time and resources pursuing that angle but, she could hardly fault him under the circumstances. If anything, it reassured her that he would leave no stone uncovered in the effort to find Melanie.

The lines on Mallory's brow softened. "Don't take it personally. It's standard procedure to verify any DNA discovered at a possible crime scene. The only way we're going to find your daughter is to follow the evidence wherever it leads and eliminate the dead ends."

Ava blinked, clutching the arm of the couch for support. His words did little to alleviate her suspicion that Mallory hadn't entirely ruled out the possibility she was somehow involved in Melanie's disappearance. The cabin was now a crime scene. By default, she was a suspect. The *prime* suspect. She had been the last one to see her daughter before she went missing. A squeaky sob escaped her lips. It was true that Melanie had been in her care, and she'd failed to keep her safe. But she hadn't intentionally done anything to harm her. Surely, Mallory didn't think she was capable of hurting her own child? She wasn't a monster by any stretch of the imagination.

One-by-one the other officers returned to the family room. "Nothing else to report, sir," Brent said. "She's not inside the cabin or anywhere else on the property. We've searched the garage and the wood shed."

Ava swallowed the hard knot in her throat. At least now maybe they would stop wasting precious time and begin tracking down her daughter in earnest. Mallory's assurance that the road blocks would stop any potential abductor fleeing the area didn't negate the possibility that someone had taken Melanie by snowmobile deep into the backcountry and used a forest service road to cross the mountains and escape. Ava had spent enough time photographing the surrounding area to know there were plenty of alternative ways to leave Brooksbury undetected.

"All right, let's get Search and Rescue underway." Mallory turned abruptly on his heel and led the officers out into the buffeting wind.

Ava followed them to the front lawn where the local SAR volunteers were assembled in front of a tall man with dark, rambling brows and a thickly-thatched beard. "I've separated the map into grids so form groups of three or four," he boomed as he handed out flyers with Melanie's picture and description in protective plastic sleeves to the men and women dressed to do battle against the worsening elements. "Each group can take one highlighted section," he continued, holding up a map and jabbing at it with his finger. When he spotted Mallory, he broke away and walked over to where he was standing.

Mallory shook his hand and then turned to Ava. "This is Justin, the area crew boss for our Search and Rescue volunteers."

Justin gave her a barely perceptible nod, his weathered face betraying no emotion as he murmured something to the sheriff. A fresh wave of guilt gripped Ava. She could tell by the look on Justin's face that he was trying hard not to appear as if he was judging her negligence, but what else could he possibly be thinking? They all must be thinking the same thing. What mother loses her four-year-old child by the shore of a frozen lake on the eve of a blizzard? The general consensus would be *a bad one*. But, they didn't really know her. None of them knew the lengths she'd gone to for Melanie's sake, or the risks she'd taken to safeguard their future—a future far from Gordon's reach.

Lost in thought, she flinched at the gentle touch of Mallory's hand on her arm. "I'm sorry to have to ask you this, but we're going to need an article of Melanie's clothing, unwashed if possible."

Ava gave a tight nod fighting the urge not to dissolve into a torrent of tears in front of everyone. She knew it was illogical, but the simple request felt more in keeping with the task of recovering a body than searching for her missing four-year-old daughter. "I'll run inside and grab something." She ducked her head, pretending to shield her face from the falling snow, but really trying to avoid the excruciating mixture of sympathetic and appraising glances from the small army of volunteers—faces she recognized from BBQ cookouts at the lake, fourth of July fireworks, church services, Christmas bazaars, and the annual craft fair where she sold her framed landscape photographs. Gulping back a sob of despair, she hurried up the front steps and into the cabin to retrieve an article of Melanie's clothing from the laundry hamper.

When she returned a few minutes later, clutching a fuzzy purple sweatshirt, it was only with trepidation that she let Mallory pry it from her gloved fingers and pass it off to Justin. Handing it over felt like an admission of guilt—a public confession of sorts that she was a failure as a mother. She was responsible for the life that had inhabited that sweatshirt as recently as yesterday, a life she had brought into the world and had not protected well enough to prevent this nightmare from taking root. She plunged her fists into her jacket pockets and watched as the volunteers split up into smaller groups. If they found Melanie wandering in the snow, Gordon would have grounds to push for full custody. She might even go to prison for child endangerment. Everything she had put into place would all have been for nothing. She shivered and tossed the disturbing thoughts aside. Melanie's safety was all that mattered now. The sooner they found her, the better. She would deal with the fallout afterward.

Armed with their plastic sleeves of information, the groups of searchers dispersed in a rustle of anticipation, accompanied by two lithe German Shepherds straining at their leashes. Moments later, the utility snowmobile roared to life.

Ava threw Mallory a harried glance. "I should go with them. Melanie will wonder where I am if they find her and I'm not there to comfort her. She'll be terrified. She knows she's not supposed to go anywhere with strangers."

"If she's unhurt, they'll likely bring her straight back here. If they elect to take her directly to the hospital for evaluation, we can meet them there." Mallory pressed his lips together and peered at her more closely. "You should make that call we talked about earlier, now that we've established Melanie's not hiding in the house or anywhere else on the property."

Ava froze, as it struck her what Mallory was referring to. She had a legal, not to mention a moral, obligation to let Gordon know their daughter was missing before he heard it from someone else. Even if it turned out that Melanie's disappearance was connected to what she'd uncovered about her husband, he still needed to be apprised of the situation. He, more than anyone, knew the gravity of the situation if it turned out that Melanie had been abducted. She pressed her nails into the palms of her hands, already dreading hearing the sound of his voice, his ongoing scathing diatribes about her inept parenting echoing in her ear. "My phone's dead," she muttered, knowing it sounded like a feeble attempt to delay the inevitable.

Wordlessly, Mallory handed her his mobile and then folded his arms across his chest, waiting for her to make the call.

Her pulse spluttered so loudly in her ears she could

scarcely hear the dial tone as she punched in Gordon's number. How was she going to break the news to him that Melanie was missing, and that it was entirely her fault? He would be livid. In his mind, what she'd allowed to happen would justify every embellished story he had ever told about her being the world's worst mother.

Gordon thought she was too weak to stand up to him, but she had gone to great lengths to make sure she would get full custody of their daughter when the time came. It had simply been too heartbreaking to imagine Gordon and Melanie spending time at the cabin without her, skipping stones together and floating on the lake in inflatable tubes. That's why she'd put all the pieces in place to make sure it never came to that. It had taken months of careful preparation, with the kind of help that came at a price, but it would be worth every penny in the end. She grimaced inwardly as she clutched the phone tighter. Losing their daughter now was not the kind of rap sheet she needed.

After several rings, the call went to voicemail. "Gordon, it's Ava. I need to talk to you. It's not about the child support. It's important. Something's happened." Her voice shook and she cleared her throat before continuing, "Call me back as soon as you get this message."

A couple of minutes later, Mallory's mobile beeped, signaling a text.

What? In a meeting. Who's phone is this?

Ava swallowed hard before punching in a reply.

Melanie is missing.

She jumped when, seconds later, Mallory's phone rang with an unfamiliar tone. "Hello?" she mumbled as she hit the speaker button.

"Are you screwing with me?" Gordon fumed. "I'm trying to get some work done here. What do you mean Melanie's missing? I'm sick of your games, Ava. What's going on now?"

She sucked a cold, calming breath through her lips before letting it flutter back out. "Our daughter disappeared this morning, that's what's going on."

Gordon groaned in disgust. "I swear you find every possible way to waste my time and wind me up. Did you check next door?"

"We're not in Cedarville. We're in Brooksbury for the weekend, remember? Clearing my stuff out of the cabin like you wanted."

For a long moment there was silence. When Gordon spoke again, his tone was heavier, more urgent. "That's a five hour drive from here. What do you want me to do about it?"

"Your daughter is missing. What do you think you should do?" Ava spat back through gritted teeth.

In the background, Gordon yelled something to his personal assistant before returning his attention to their conversation. "You can't be trusted with anything. I can't believe you. How did you lose her? Maybe she walked to my mother's."

"I checked there. Your mother's—"

"—in Chicago. I know that, but Melanie might have forgotten. Where did you see her last—can you even remember that much?"

Ava stared at the phone in her hand, fighting the urge to fling it across the room, cognizant that Mallory was watching—not to mention the fact that it was his phone. "We were walking by the lake this morning. I was taking pictures of the ski runs and she wanted to run ahead, like she always does. When I looked up, she was gone."

"What do you mean *gone*?" The snap in Gordon's voice indicated he had abandoned all pretense at patience. "How can she be gone? Are you seriously telling me you lost our daughter at the lake while you zoned out with your stupid camera? How do you know she didn't drown?"

"Get a grip, Gordon!" Ava retorted. "Of course she didn't drown. The lake's still frozen over. I only took a few quick pictures and when I looked up, she'd disappeared."

She flinched when Gordon yelled through the phone, "And you call yourself a mother! You're useless! Always with your face stuck in your phone or behind a camera, never paying the slightest bit of attention to our daughter! Tell you what, why don't you post a missing photo of her on your Instagram? Maybe your so-called friends on social media will find her for us. You're a sorry excuse for a parent, Ava! Believe me, you'll never get custody as long as there's breath in my lungs!"

Ava clenched her jaw, bracing herself against the verbal barrage as Gordon continued to spew, making no attempt to listen to what she was saying, or offer any measure of compassion for what she was going through. But, she hadn't expected anything different. Not from a narcissist like him.

Mallory gestured for the phone. "Let me talk to him."

Ava thrust the mobile gratefully into the sheriff's palm and walked over to the kitchen counter to plug in her own phone to charge. She leaned against the counter, eyes downcast, listening in on the ongoing conversation.

"Hey, Gordon, Mallory Anderson here."

Gordon let out an indignant sputter. "Please tell me you're not involved in this investigation."

"As a matter of fact, I'm leading it up."

Mallory stared impassively at the screen while Gordon unloaded an earful about the incompetence of police in rural parts. When the rant died down, Mallory continued in a measured tone, "I'm going to have to ask you to come up to Brooksbury and assist us in the search for your daughter."

There was a beat of silence and then Gordon responded in a more subdued pitch, "How long has she been missing? Have you even started looking for her?"

"SAR crews have just been dispatched."

"She can't have gone far. My wife's completely inept. There's no sense in me jumping in the car just yet. I'm right in the middle of an important negotiation. You'll probably find her in the next few minutes."

Mallory briefly caught Ava's eye and grimaced. She could tell by the strained look on his face that he didn't want her overhearing what he was gearing up to say next. His voice quieted as he went on, "That's assuming Melanie's lost, Gordon. If someone's taken her, she could be a lot further away by now than any of us know."

Ava scrunched her eyes shut and inhaled and exhaled slowly, her head pounding with a torrent of sickening thoughts. She shouldn't have risked coming back to Brooksbury. She should have disappeared in a city bustling with strangers. That way she would never have let go of Melanie's hand to begin with.

4

*A*va stared resentfully as her estranged husband entered the cabin, immaculately turned out as always in a well-tailored black wool coat. The withering scowl she had grown accustomed to over the years intersected his pale face as he drummed his fingers on the kitchen counter. She was supposed to be enjoying a final weekend at the lake free of this pathological liar of a man she'd married —a businessman without scruples, and a philanderer without a conscience as it turned out. She'd been the last person to find out that he'd cheated on her in their first year of marriage with his newly-hired, buxom, twenty-one-year-old PA. Despite the devastating betrayal, Ava had naively tried her best to patch things up and make a go of their marriage. She'd even gone to counseling for close to a year regardless of the fact that Gordon refused to join her.

When she got pregnant with Melanie, she'd dared to believe their marriage would survive the fallout from the affair. She'd actually allowed herself to think they could become one of those families who had a secret handshake, and special names for each other—the kind of family who flicked through photo albums together every December in matching ugly Christmas sweaters, and notched growth charts into the wall, and buried time capsules in the back yard. But, it turned out they were the type of family who found hiding places to bury their secrets in. Except Gordon hadn't hidden his secrets all that well after all. She was doing a much better job of it.

In the years following Melanie's birth, things between them had only deteriorated. Ava had wanted to try for another child—Melanie often begged for a little brother or sister—but Gordon flatly refused. As if to ensure there was no possible way it could happen, he spent every spare minute at work, or in Brooksbury, purportedly visiting his mother, and rarely saw Melanie who was fast asleep when he left for the office each morning, and back in bed by the time he arrived home in the evening, if he showed up at all. He adamantly denied having another affair, but he treated Ava like a cross between an unwanted expenditure on his balance sheet and a live-in nanny. She didn't have the heart to keep pumping anything more into her deflating expectations. When she'd eventually plucked up the courage to ask for a divorce, Gordon had threatened to kill her. And knowing what she did about him now, she had little doubt that he had the connections to make her death look like an unfortunate accident.

Melanie's disappearance had upset all Ava's plans to leave Gordon, filling her with the kind of terror she'd only ever imagined a parent could experience. The last thing she'd expected to find herself doing at the cabin this weekend was searching for her daughter with Gordon. His presence here only drove home the harsh reality that Melanie had now been missing for almost seven hours. In typical Gordon fashion, he'd insisted on waiting a full hour before finally leaving work and making the drive up to Brooksbury. Ava found it nauseating, but not surprising, that he could continue to bury himself in his work knowing his only child was missing. The expression on Mallory's face when Gordon relayed his intentions over the phone told her he found it just as deplorable. It was really a shame Mallory didn't have any children of his own. He would have made a great father. She could tell by the tender look in his eyes when he talked about Melanie that he had a soft spot for kids. She only wished she'd been savvy enough to recognize that in a man before she'd married Gordon.

"The light will start fading soon," Gordon snapped, throwing Mallory an accusatory stare as he hung up his coat and scarf on the rack by the door. "What's your plan?"

Mallory rubbed his jaw. "As you know, there's a storm coming in, but the volunteers will continue to search as long as it's safe to do so. The dogs can track equally as well at night, and Justin has lined up replacement volunteers and rescue dogs for when they tire."

"We wouldn't be needing to line up replacements if you'd done your job and found my daughter already," Gordon fired back.

"Rest assured, we're doing everything we can," Mallory replied.

Gordon smoothed a hand over his bald head, pacing back and forth in a hand-stitched gray designer suit with tortoise shell buttons. "Could she even survive out here at night? I mean she's only four-years-old. What's she supposed to do, build a shelter?"

"She's dressed appropriately for the weather," Mallory responded in a measured tone. "That's a good start. Naturally we're still holding out hope that we'll find her before night falls and the temperature drops."

Gordon snorted and glared at Ava. "Well at least you managed to dress her properly before you lost her."

"That's not fair, Gordon, and you know it." She flashed him a sharp look. "How many times have you lost sight of her—like that day at the park when you were so engrossed in your phone you didn't notice she'd climbed into another family's car. They were about to take her to the police station."

"Don't be so dramatic!" Gordon growled, his tone laced with disgust. "She wandered over to chat with some other kids for a couple of minutes. That's what kids do if you took the time to notice."

"She was only two-years-old! And she was with the family for forty-five minutes, Gordon. They searched everywhere for you."

Mallory cleared his throat. "Let's try and stay focused, shall we? Like I said, if conditions allow, the search will continue through the night with fresh volunteers. In the meantime, we've erected roadblocks on the only road leading in and out of Brooksbury. We're stopping every car and asking if anyone has seen Melanie or any suspicious strangers or unfamiliar vehicles in the area. Another thing you might want to consider is offering a reward for any information, assuming you're in a position to bankroll it."

Gordon narrowed his eyes. "Money's not an issue, it's your department's ineptitude that concerns me."

Ignoring the dig, Mallory turned to Ava and asked, "Is Melanie afraid of the dark?"

Ava shook her head, her eyes filling up with tears again at the tenderness in Mallory's voice. "She's more afraid of strangers after the incident at the park. I scared her into never talking to another stranger. I'm certain she wouldn't have gone willingly with someone she didn't know."

Gordon's phone dinged and he pulled it out and frowned at it. He scrolled through a lengthy message and then began punching out a text in response.

Ava grimaced. Was he actually trying to conduct business when his daughter was out there somewhere in the cold, lost and terrified? Or was he just trying to make himself look important in front of Mallory. For some reason he seemed intent on treating the man like he was a rival instead of an ally.

After an uncomfortable silence, Gordon slid his phone back into his pocket and fixed a cold stare on Mallory. "What if it wasn't a stranger who took my daughter? Have you considered the possibility that someone in Brooksbury might be behind Melanie's disappearance? Someone who knew her? Are you questioning the residents?"

Mallory bristled and adjusted the brim of his hat. "At this point, we haven't ruled out anyone." He stared pointedly back at Gordon.

Ava detected a nerve twitch in her estranged husband's neck. She bit her lip, furrowing her brow. Could Gordon have had something to do with Melanie's disappearance? She quickly dismissed the theory. It made no sense. He didn't know she'd found out everything he'd been hiding from her. Besides, he'd been hundreds of miles away, doing what Gordon did best, wheeling and dealing. True, he hadn't been consistent with his child support of late, but it wasn't because he couldn't afford the payments. He was doing it to punish her. Striving to make her life difficult to get her back for threatening to seek full custody of Melanie. Gordon was a man who liked to be in control. And, until now, he had been. If only he knew how badly out of control his world was about to spin.

5

*D*arkness finally fell on the longest day of her life, and Ava pulled on a heavy sweater, flinching at the sound of the wind hurling itself against the cabin like a violent predator. She slumped despondently down on the couch and tucked her legs beneath her, imagining Melanie curled up against a snow bank in a futile attempt to hide her thin limbs from the ravages of the storm. She wished with all her heart there was some way to transmit the heat of her body to her daughter, she would willingly give up the last degree of warmth in her own blood to preserve her sweet child's life. Everything she had put in place over the past several months had been with Melanie's long-term safety in mind. But, they might not have a future together after this. If Melanie had been abducted, she could be hundreds of miles away by now. And if she was still out there somewhere, her lips would be blue by now, her tiny, turned-up nose red as raw meat, tears streaming down her little face. Ava wondered briefly if tears could freeze. She brushed a hand across her own eyes, longing to feel a comforting arm around her, giving her the strength to keep believing. As if determined to aggravate her, Gordon paced across the rug in front of the couch, glancing at his watch repeatedly and stroking his ridiculous attempt at a goatee—a nod to his newly reinstated bachelor status—not that he'd ever abandoned it in practice.

Ava's phone vibrated in her sweater pocket. She pulled it out, her heartbeat picking up pace when she saw who was calling. "Hi, Aunt Delia," she said, striking an upbeat tone as she got to her feet and made her way to the master bedroom. She closed the door behind her and leaned her back against it. "What do you want?" she hissed.

"Code name *Aunt Delia*. That's brilliant, that is. Do I knit, too?"

"Very funny. It's the first name that came into my head."

"Do you have an Aunt Delia?"

"What do you want?"

"I take it you can't talk?"

"I can now," Ava muttered. "But not for long. Why are you calling me? You got your money. I got what I needed. Have you left town yet?"

"No, I was hired to do another job so I decided to stick around."

A prickling heat crawled the length of Ava's spine. An intuition of sorts. Her voice sank to a breathless whisper. "What kind of a job?"

"I think you know."

Ava gasped and clamped a hand to her mouth. "Melanie?"

"Yeah."

"Who ... who put you up to this?"

"It was her."

Confusion flooded Ava's brain. "I don't understand. Why?"

She sank down to the floor and listened in shocked silence to the low murmuring on the other end of the line. It was hard to believe what she was hearing at first, but the longer she listened, the more it all began to make sense. Gordon had seriously underestimated all three of the women in his life.

Slowly, a radical idea took shape in Ava's head. All was not lost. She could use this twist to salvage her original plan —improve on it even, take them all down in one fell swoop if she played her cards right and bided her time. When the voice on the other end fell silent, she relayed a series of whispered instructions, with the promise of additional cash, before ending the call.

Getting to her feet, she took some time to contemplate her next steps, before dialing another number. It was time to tell the real Aunt Delia what had happened and enlist her help.

AN HOUR OR SO LATER, the door to the cabin opened and Justin's solid frame filled the doorway, his beard frosted with a dusting of snow.

"Any news?" Ava feigned a hoarse whisper as she got to her feet. She felt incredibly guilty knowing the volunteers would be combing the frozen lake all night for nothing, but she desperately needed to buy more time. It was important to stay in character as the distraught mother of a missing child for the next twenty-four hours at least. She only hoped it wouldn't take any longer than that. Her heart was already aching beyond what she could bear. She needed to be with her daughter again, to know for sure that she was safe and unharmed. Nothing was a given when the stakes were this high.

Justin shook his head gravely. "No trace of her. Estimates are we're going to get upwards of thirty inches overnight. If visibility goes down to nothing, I'm going to recommend we call off the search until morning."

"No! Absolutely not!" Gordon snapped, striding over to the door. "Do your job! You need to stay out there and keep searching until you find my daughter. That's when you can call off the search, and not a minute before." He adjusted the cuff of his jacket sleeve, blinking nervously when Justin drew himself up to his full height, eyes glinting with something deep and dangerous.

"We can't accomplish anything if we can't see through the blizzard," Justin responded stiffly. "I understand your frustration as a parent, but I won't risk endangering the lives of my volunteers. They have families to consider too. We'll keep searching only as long as it's safe to do so." He thrust a stainless steel thermos against Gordon's chest. "In the meantime, why don't you busy yourself brewing some fresh coffee for the volunteers braving the elements on your behalf." Without waiting for a response, Justin turned and strode back out through the front door, letting it slam behind him.

Gordon eyed with displeasure the creeping coffee stain on his pressed, white shirt. He tossed the thermos into the sink with a disgruntled protest before turning to address Mallory, "I take it you sanctioned that unprofessional oaf to lead the volunteers. He's nothing more than a two-legged wildebeest!"

"You ought to be thankful you have a mountain man on your team," Mallory retorted. "It'll take one to find your daughter once it starts dumping hard tonight. No one knows this terrain better than Justin."

"Yeah, well, so far he's got squat to show for his wealth of knowledge," Gordon scoffed.

"I can't stay here and do nothing all evening while the volunteers are searching," Ava said. "Surely there must be something we can do to help. I know it's windy out there but it's only snowing lightly so far."

Mallory rubbed a hand over his jaw. "We could take a drive and talk to some of the neighbors. It's possible someone might have found Melanie wandering by the lake and picked her up earlier not knowing who she belonged to. With the storm coming in, they might not want to risk driving into Brooksbury, and cell service is spotty at the best of times around the lake."

He turned to Gordon. "Do you want to come with us or wait here?"

"I'll stay at the cabin." He arched a condescending brow at Ava. "One of us needs to be here for our daughter. Stable environment and all that."

Ava opened her mouth to respond but Mallory cut her off. "Let's go before this storm really kicks up."

Ava grabbed her jacket from the coat rack by the door. Something about Mallory's tone told her he wasn't referring to the weather.

SHE SHIVERED as she pulled the door of the squad car shut and brushed the snowflakes from her hair. "So where are we headed to first?"

"May and Walt Ward's place. It's the closest residence to yours this side of the lake. They moved back to the area last summer. He's a retired contractor. Do you know them?"

Ava's heart began to drum in her chest. She nodded, keeping her eyes forward. "I know who they are. I've never actually met them—" Her voice trailed off. It was true she hadn't run into them yet, but she knew only too well why they'd moved away in the first place. Best not to say too much. She didn't want Mallory bringing up the subject of their delinquent son—Jeremy Ward—without whom she'd never have discovered Gordon's secrets, or obtained the evidence she needed to ensure he wouldn't get custody of Melanie.

It had been a chance encounter last spring. She'd been hiking in the backcountry, camera in tow as always. Gordon had taken Melanie to his mother's house to bake some cookies. Jeremy had been engrossed in checking his game camera when she'd stumbled across him the first time. Maybe they'd clicked over their love of photographing wildlife or maybe it was over their shared hatred of Gordon—probably a little of both. Over the course of several conversations, Ava learned that her husband had been the reason Jeremy had gone to jail in 2011 for four years. Gordon had hired him for a job, then set him up to take the fall when things went sideways. Unsurprisingly, Jeremy had been more than willing to oblige Ava's seemingly benign request for a reasonable fee. It had turned out to be a far more valuable relationship than she could ever have imagined. But it was imperative Mallory stayed in the dark about their arrangement. She couldn't allow all her carefully laid plans to unravel.

"We haven't been coming up here a lot lately," Ava explained. "So I haven't had an opportunity to socialize with the Wards yet. I believe May Ward was Gordon's high school English teacher."

Mallory grunted. "We all had her."

Ava raised an eyebrow. "She taught you too?"

Mallory chortled. "She tried her best. I wasn't exactly a model student to put it mildly."

"You can't have been a lost cause entirely. You graduated the police academy."

"Let's just say criminal justice was a lot more interesting than King Lear."

Ava let out a despondent sigh. "They're equally depressing."

Mallory threw her a guilt-ridden look. She could tell he was kicking himself for his tactless reference to a Shakespearean tragedy about someone getting lost in a thunderstorm. She felt horrible about loading on the guilt unnecessarily but she couldn't rouse Mallory's suspicions. Tonight he needed to believe she was a bereft parent, desperate to be reunited with her daughter—a role she could play to perfection.

"It's always that much tougher when there's a child involved," Mallory empathized, as they pulled up outside a modest single family home with a wraparound porch flanked by a steel-sided workshop and a smaller, slightly dilapidated storage shed. "But I can honestly say there's no better tracker in these parts than Justin. If anyone can find your daughter, he can."

Ava dabbed at her eyes for effect. "Melanie isn't just *a* child, she's *my* child. Justin may be a reputable tracker but, let's face it, he hasn't come up with a single lead after searching for her all afternoon. She could be lost, dead, or kidnapped for all he knows."

"I'm sorry," Mallory said with a note of regret in his voice. "I didn't mean to upset you."

Ava shook her head in dramatic fashion. "It's not your fault. I just wish now that I hadn't left her and gone into town to get help. Maybe if I'd stayed and searched a little longer I would have found her."

Mallory reached out a hand and squeezed her shoulder gently. "You did what any good mother would have done. You acted in your child's best interests. There's no benefit to second-guessing yourself now."

A tear trickled down Ava's cheek at the welcome affirmation of her parenting. "You've been so kind through all of this," she said. "I mean that most sincerely." She fished out a bedraggled tissue and blew her nose before gesturing to the house. "Let's get this over with."

A SHRUNKEN MAN with drooping eyes and an elongated bald head opened the weathered front door after Mallory had thumped on it for a few minutes. At the man's side stood a gray-muzzled black lab, wagging its tail tentatively.

"Evening, Walt," Mallory said. "Can we come in? Melanie Galbraith has gone missing and we're canvassing the neighbors hoping someone might have seen her or noticed something that could lead us to her."

A nervous flicker crossed Walt's face. "Gordon's daughter. Oh my, that's awful. Come on in, please." He cast a rheumy-eyed glance over Ava before ushering both her and Mallory into a narrow hall. They followed him over the creaking floorboards into a cozy sitting room heated by a wood stove. Walt sat down heavily on a sagging butterscotch-colored couch next to a thin, unmoving woman with skin like ruffled fabric, hands folded neatly in her lap.

Mallory and Ava seated themselves on matching floral wingback accent chairs facing the couch.

"Evening, Mrs. Ward," Mallory said in a jovial tone.

May Ward turned to her husband. "Who is that man?"

Walt patted her hand gently and then smiled benignly at Mallory. "May has dementia. She doesn't remember you. Some days she doesn't even remember me. It can be very frightening for her." He turned to Ava. "Visitors are even more unsettling." He blinked, and Ava wasn't sure if he was reprimanding her or soliciting sympathy.

She gave a tight smile. "I'm so sorry to hear that," she said, forcing the words through her lips. Truth be told, she was too numb from the trauma of the day to feel a whole lot of empathy for her elderly neighbor's lost memories. May Ward had already lived a long life. Melanie, on the other hand, was only four-years-old and needed her mother. Ava wasn't sure her nerves would hold out for much longer. She threw a harried glance at Mallory, her expression clearly conveying that they were wasting time here—willing him to say something to that effect—but his attention was firmly fixed on May Ward.

"Mrs. Ward, this is Ava Galbraith, Gordon's wife," Mallory spelled out in the same patient tone he had used with Ava when he'd taken her statement down at the station. "She's staying at their cabin for the weekend. She and her daughter, Melanie, went for a walk this morning down by the lake and Melanie has gone missing. We stopped by on the off chance that she might have wandered this way."

May remained unresponsive, her eyes fixed on a matted patch of the variegated carpet that looked like it was designed to camouflage every variant shade of pet stain and beverage spill on the color wheel.

After an uncomfortable silence, Walt cleared his throat. "May scarcely talks to anyone but me these days. I haven't seen Melanie but then I haven't been out all day. I don't get out much anymore, not even to my workshop. I usually go to the market on Thursdays but with the storm forecast I went yesterday instead and stocked up on groceries." He shifted position on the couch, rubbing his palms on his pant legs. "Sometimes the storm rolls in earlier than they predict. These meteorologists never can seem to get it right."

Ava studied him with interest as he prattled on. She knew exactly why he was acting so nervous. She'd seen it in his eyes the moment he'd opened the door to them and Mallory had told him Melanie was missing. He was afraid of what his son might have done this time, the son who wasn't supposed to be here.

"Did you see anyone at all today?" Mallory inquired.

"What did he say?" May asked too loudly.

Walt patted her hand again, ignoring her question, "Only Jim Stewart, the postman."

Mallory pulled out his notebook. "What time was that at?"

Walt smoothed a hand over the fuzz on the crown of his head. "I want to say around two this afternoon. That's his usual time."

"Did he mention anything out of the ordinary?"

Walt furrowed his brow. "No, I don't believe so. We talked about the storm some. He was aiming to finish his route early and get on home."

Mallory nodded and scribbled a note on the pad resting on his knee before getting to his feet. "I'll give him a call anyway. Thanks for your time, Walt."

"He shouldn't have come back." May's reedy voice wafted through the room, her eyes suddenly alert.

A cold shiver shot down Ava's spine. *She knows!*

"Sorry about that," Walt muttered, looking flustered. "She talks gibberish every now and then, sometimes says very inappropriate things. She doesn't realize she's doing it."

"He's here," May insisted.

"Who's here?" Mallory asked.

"Please, don't stress her out," Walt pleaded, stroking the back of his wife's hands. "She gets upset when she's confused and it takes a long time to get her calmed down again. Sometimes we're up half the night before she settles down."

Mallory walked across to the couch and hunkered down in front of May. "Was someone other than the postman here, Mrs. Ward?"

She hung her head and said nothing, making a strange, growling sound at the back of her throat.

Walt scratched his neck and gave a small shrug. "She must be talking about Jim, no one else stopped by today."

"Not Jim." May lifted her head and stared straight ahead, her brow rumpled in concentration.

Walt laid a hand on his wife's arm but she shrugged him off and got to her feet unsteadily. She hobbled over to the window and pointed to the yard outside. "He parked his truck out front."

Walt raised amused brows at Mallory and Ava as he addressed his wife, "That's right, May. Jim always parks the postal truck there. He brought a letter from our granddaughter, remember?"

"He came by yesterday when you went into town." May's voice quieted to a whisper. "He went into the workshop. I told him he shouldn't have come back."

6

*She hummed to herself as she screwed the shiny plastic lid
back on the bottle of velvet berry nail polish after
touching up a chip that had been irritating her all day long. Ah,
much better. She liked an orderly world—the illusion of perfection.
Goals and standards were so terribly important after all. It was too
easy to let things slide, to compromise on the rules she needed to
stick to—more importantly, that others needed to abide by. People
had a bad habit of abandoning the playbook when the heat was
turned up. That's when everything inevitably started spinning out
of control.*

*It was frustrating when people ignored her advice, or called her
perspective into question, but she always managed to turn things
around in her favor in the end. People dismissed her far too easily.
If only they knew what she was capable of. Granted, things with
Gordon were not as they should be right now, but she had a fool-
proof plan to remedy that situation. A grin tugged at her glossed
lips. She would have made an excellent project manager with her
multi-tasking skills. She took a quick picture of the nail polish with
her phone to remind herself to pick up another bottle of velvet*

berry, before replacing it in her vanity drawer. Even the barista at the coffee shop had gushed about the color when she'd reached for her latte yesterday.

Things were all working out beautifully, better than she could possibly have hoped for under the trying circumstances. She had become adept at persuading people to see what she wanted them to see, a survival mechanism of sorts when life backhanded your dreams in the worst kind of way. Enveloped in the comforting warmth of her success felt so much better than being wrapped in Gordon's arms ever had. Patricia had taken the bait so readily. The fool knew it was wrong on some level, but she was so desperate to keep her son and granddaughter in her iron embrace that she was prepared to rationalize her ill-advised actions after a little gentle persuasion.

She let out an amused snort. Patricia Galbraith didn't believe she was good enough for her son. If only Patricia knew just how good she'd been for Gordon all these years. Bringing the Galbraith matriarch to her knees would be an enjoyable bonus. Payback for everything Patricia had put her through had been a long time coming. Still, she needed to stay focused on the more important task at hand. It was time to put the rest of her plan into action.

Satisfied that her rehabbed nail was perfectly dry, she picked up her phone and dialed.

"Yeah?" A loud yawn accompanied the gruff greeting.

"You sound discomposed," she purred. "Did I disturb your beauty sleep?"

"I haven't got time for mind games. What do you want?"

"You've got a green light."

"You mean ... tonight?"

She let out an aggrieved sigh, angling her fingers in front of her to study the plane of her nails. Was that a bump she detected? Irritation crept into her voice. "We've been over this already? What do you think a green light means?"

"No need to get all bent out of shape. This is business. We've been down this road together before. Just making sure it's time to play ball."

"Hence the call," she replied, rolling her eyes. She had grown weary of his unrelenting stupidity. She was no longer the same woman he had known growing up. They had been equals as children, but everything had changed in the intervening years. He had certain attributes that still made him useful, but their paths had diverged years ago. A yawning chasm separated them now. She had played her cards right and ridden out the storm when it hit, but he had folded and paid the price.

Gordon was nothing like him. She came alive in a primal way in Gordon's company. Their conversation sparkled, granted with a few daggers thrown in, but she liked the danger in the world they had created together. In the end, she and Gordon worked well as a team. A homing attraction always brought him back to her in the end. This time would be no different. She had a plan to iron out the one tiny wrinkle that kept them apart.

"And the money?" the rough voice on the other end of the call demanded.

"The money will be where we agreed it would be, after I get the picture confirming the job has been completed to my satisfaction."

"You'll get it. Some time tonight. Don't know exactly when."

"Excellent, I look forward to receiving it." Extending her fingers again, she studied the nails she had finished painting moments earlier. Such a beautiful color, a flawless collusion of brilliant and rich. It suited her. Her brilliance was going to make her rich, she sensed it like a predator senses the racing heart of its prey. She only needed to persevere a little longer. She wet her lips, choosing her next words carefully. "And you're sure no one saw you?"

"Naw, just the old lady. We're good."

"Very well, don't call me again until you have the confirmation picture. After that we'll go our separate ways, for good this time."

She ended the call, set her phone on the vanity counter and frowned at her reflection in the mirror.

Technically May Walt wasn't no one. She was a straggly thread that could unravel everything.

7

*P*atricia Galbraith stared down adoringly at her sleeping granddaughter, her creamy complexion flushed against a backdrop of dark ringlets spread out over the silk pillowcase in the ornate sleigh bed in her guest bedroom. Gordon's child was perfect in every way, just as he had been at her age. A tiny furrow of consternation crossed Patricia's brow. He was a good son to her, but she worried sometimes about the stress he was under running the business he had inherited from his father. She didn't understand much about investments or financial planning, but Gordon certainly seemed to have made a roaring success of it. Her husband had provided reasonably well for her when he was alive, but Gordon had taken things to a whole new level. Considering the fact that he had only ever been an average student in school, he had surpassed her wildest expectations.

Patrica checked her watch for the umpteenth time. The sleeping pill she had given Melanie in her mug of hot chocolate a short while ago, would knock her out for several hours. With a bit of luck it would leave her too disoriented to remember how and when she had arrived at her grandmother's house, which would be for the best. Patricia pulled her lips into a satisfied smile. She had done an excellent job of explaining to Melanie how a concerned friend had found her wandering alone at the lake that morning and driven her to Gammy's house. She'd actually cried when she told Melanie how fortunate she'd been that a nice lady had found her and not some bad person. "Mommy was so busy taking photographs she forgot all about you. Not to worry, sweetheart," Patricia had soothed, as she dabbed at the corner of her eyes with a tissue, careful not to mess up her makeup. "Gammy will make you some hot chocolate to warm your tummy and then we'll call Mommy. I'm sure she will be very sorry she lost you."

Melanie had blinked solemnly and accepted the explanation without question, before trotting off down the hall to the well-stocked toy box in the guest room. While she was happily occupied talking to her favorite stuffed animals, Patricia warmed the milk for the drugged hot chocolate. Ava would be beside herself with worry, but it was important that she learn her lesson. It was also important that Melanie was missing long enough to justify involving the police—Ava's negligence needed to be well documented by the proper authorities.

Ava had hammered on Patricia's front door earlier that morning, but she hadn't hung around for long, no doubt believing her mother-in-law was still in Chicago. Patrica knew Ava had gone directly to the police station after that. As promised, her informant was keeping her apprised of the situation as it developed and making sure she stayed one step ahead of the investigation. So far, everything was going according to plan.

Patricia gently brushed an errant curl from Melanie's forehead. She was the spitting image of Gordon in photos at this age—she could have been his twin. Thankfully, she bore no resemblance to Ava with her thin, limp hair, whiny voice and permanently startled expression. Patricia grimaced. She had hoped her daughter-in-law would be a malleable addition to the Galbraith family, serving in a supporting role as Gordon's success grew. She had grudgingly accepted Ava into the family as the lesser of two evils—the greater being Tammy Bates who had pursued Gordon aggressively in high school, zeroing in on him as her ticket out of the trailer park.

Given the fact that Ava's aunt, Delia Marsh, was a renowned research oncologist, while Tammy's father, Fred Bates, had been in and out of prison more times than anyone could count, Patricia had deemed Ava's pedigree the more favorable of the two. But, despite Tammy's undesirable roots, for some frustrating reason, Gordon remained smitten with her all through high school. Patricia had seen straight through her from the outset—a money-grubbing miscreant who was lucky enough to be endowed with a brain along with her arresting looks. A dangerous combination that Gordon found irresistible. It had necessitated a loving mother's intervention to save him. Patricia had viewed the somewhat dull but well bred Ava, the more suitable wife, and, after a considerable amount of persuasion, and a fair share of pressure in regard to his inheritance, Gordon had reluctantly come to the same conclusion.

Patricia pursed her lips when she recalled the troubling conversation last Christmas when Gordon informed her that Ava was filing for divorce. A white-hot anger still burned in Patricia's gut every time she thought about it. How dare that insipid woman try to destroy him after everything he had done for her. From the outset, he had showered her with lavish gifts and vacations, and catered to her every whim. He gave her the wedding of her dreams, and even let her hire a renowned designer to plan a nursery when she fell pregnant with Melanie. Regardless of the prenup, Ava might be able to get her greedy paws on more of her son's money than Patricia would like, but she was going to make sure she didn't win custody of Melanie. By the time she called the sheriff's office to let them know that her missing four-year-old granddaughter had been found wandering unsupervised halfway around the lake, everyone in Brooksbury would know that Ava Galbraith was a negligent and unfit mother.

Patricia's cell phone vibrated and she glanced at the screen before pressing the phone to her ear. "Hi Tammy," she whispered.

"I take it the little cherub is still sleeping?"

Patricia recoiled at the simpering tone on the other end of the call. Tammy Anderson, as she was now known, still grated on her nerves after all these years, her trailer park accent detectable despite the accent modification classes she'd taken. Nonetheless, she had her uses, not the least of which was the fact that she was married to the local sheriff, a straight-laced sort who had a reputation for coming down hard on anyone who hurt or endangered a child.

"Yes," Patricia replied. "The sleeping pill knocked her out right away. She'll be out of it for a few hours."

Patricia slipped quietly out of the guest bedroom, closed the door behind her, and made her way down the hallway to the kitchen. "How long should I wait before I call Mallory?"

"Wait until she wakes up," Tammy advised her. "Maybe until mid-afternoon. This needs to be an incident the court will take seriously if you want to make a case for negligence and child endangerment. Besides, you need to drive a stake of terror into that irresponsible woman's heart to teach her a lesson."

Patricia grimaced. "Trust me, I intend to." She pressed her lips into a disapproving line as she sat down at the table and retrieved the cup of lukewarm Earl Grey tea she had made for herself earlier. She couldn't remember exactly when

Tammy had taken it upon herself to stop addressing her as Mrs. Galbraith. It irritated her no end, but she would have to overlook it, at least until this was all over. She needed Tammy on her side long enough to see things through to a favorable conclusion. "I'm just worried about making Gordon suffer needlessly in the meantime. I hate to see him hurting."

Tammy made a sympathetic sound. "Believe me, if there was any other way to accomplish what you want, I'd direct you down that path."

Patricia smoothed a hand over her bob. "I hope you're right about this being enough to swing custody in Gordon's favor."

"Without a doubt," Tammy said firmly. "No family court judge will look favorably on an incident like this involving a full scale SAR deployment. Not to mention the fact that Ava doesn't have a real job and can't possibly afford child care given the terms of their prenup."

Patricia let out a satisfied sigh. "And of course I'm available to help Gordon raise Melanie. I can even move into the guest house on their property in Cedarville and rent this place out. Ava never wanted any part of me living in their guest house, but Gordon was always very much in favor of the idea of Melanie having her grandmother living close by."

"It's an excellent suggestion," Tammy agreed. "The judge will approve. Family members are always preferred over paid caretakers, and the fact that you're a retired nurse will only bolster Gordon's case."

"How long will it take Mallory to send someone out to investigate Ava once I make the report?" Patricia asked.

"Believe me, he'll jump right on it," Tammy soothed. "As you know, Mallory is passionate about protecting kids from abuse and neglect. He'll have child protective services crawling all over that woman before she knows what hit her.

In fact, I wouldn't be surprised if they ask Gordon to come and pick Melanie up. Ava may not be allowed any more unsupervised contact with her daughter before she goes to court."

"Really?" A tingle of anticipation crossed Patricia's shoulders at the sheer perfection of it—just her and Gordon and Melanie, the way she had always wanted it. She twisted a strand of silver hair around her finger. Of course, she would have to change her phone number afterward to get rid of Tammy and her not-so-subtle attempts to worm her way back into Gordon's life, but that was a minor issue. Patricia had known from the outset precisely why Tammy was going out of her way to help her. Tammy still had her sights set on Gordon even after all these years. Once the divorce was finalized, Patricia had no doubt Tammy would make her move. But, Patricia would do what it took to protect her son as she had always done. She took a small sip of her tea, choosing her words carefully. "You know, I really do appreciate all your help with this, Tammy. I wouldn't have had a clue how to go about it."

"It's the least I can do. Poor little Melanie." Tammy sighed before adding, "Mallory and I tried for years to have kids before we gave up. I think it's because of our own struggles that it pains us so much more to see Ava poisoning Melanie's relationship with her father. Only a sad, needy person would deprive a child of a loving father."

Patricia clenched the phone tighter in her hand. "Sad and needy certainly sums her up. If it wasn't for Gordon's social circle she would have no friends at all. She lives vicariously through that Instagram account of hers."

"It is rather pathetic how she feels the need to respond to every single comment on her photos, talking to complete strangers like they're her besties, always fishing for compliments," Tammy said. "It's sad to see a grown woman who needs an audience all the time, but can't even pay attention to her own child."

Patricia curled her lip. "I suspect she's rather a disappointment to her Aunt Delia. That woman had a brilliant mind and a very successful career by all accounts."

"It must have been so draining for Gordon being married to such a self-absorbed woman all these years."

"It still is, as long as they're both living on the same property," Patricia fumed. "Gordon wants to sell but Ava wants to keep their house in Cedarville in return for letting him have the cabin. Can you believe her gall? That wasn't part of the prenup. Besides, the cabin's been in the Galbraith family for over a hundred years. What judge in their right mind would award any part of it to her?"

Tammy tutted her disgust. "Don't worry, it can only work in Gordon's favor. It's obvious that Ava is greedy as well as negligent, not a good mother for little Melanie as her actions clearly demonstrate."

Patricia traced a fingertip around the gilt edge of her bone china tea cup, feeling somewhat vindicated. "And that's why I took your advice."

"You made the right choice for Melanie's sake—exposing her mother's true colors. It's plain to be seen now that it's too dangerous for Melanie to be left in her care any longer."

Patricia frowned at her tea. "She'll be exposed all right as soon as I make that call and Mallory alerts child protective services."

"Like I said, give it until this afternoon. We'll talk again once Melanie wakes up. I'll walk you through the word track before you make the call."

After Tammy hung up, Patricia set down her phone and took another sip of cold tea before giving up on it. The house was gloomy with all the shades pulled tight. It was too risky to turn on any lights in case she inadvertently alerted someone to the fact that she had returned early from Chicago. The last thing she needed was for Mallory or Gordon to come knocking on her door before she could make that all-important phone call. She took her cup and saucer over to the sink and rinsed them off, and then went into the laundry room at the back of the house to unload the dryer. She had taken a chance running it, but the vent wasn't visible from the road. Twenty minutes later, she hung Melanie's outerwear on the coatrack by the door and then carried a stack of neatly folded sheets back to the linen closet in the hallway to put them away.

Before heading back up to the kitchen, she quietly opened the door to the guest bedroom and peeked around it to check on Melanie. A dull thumping in her chest grew more insistent with every fleeting second as she stared uncomprehendingly at the rumpled covers on the empty bed.

8

*M*allory couldn't help but notice Ava's intense discomfort when May Ward suddenly turned away from the window she was standing in front of and locked eyes with her. For a fleeting moment, it almost appeared as if they were having a silent conversation about something only they were privy to. Did Ava know what May was talking about—who the man was she'd seen entering Walt's workshop yesterday? Mallory quickly shook off the notion. May Ward wasn't capable of having a logical conversation with her own shadow. Besides, he wasn't convinced May had seen anyone on the property to begin with. She could just be rambling. And, if Walt was to be believed, she did a lot of that.

Ava's discomfort was understandable. Even the slightest possibility that an unidentified male had been spotted in the vicinity the day before her four-year-old daughter disappeared was enough to strike terror in any mother's heart. Even Mallory was sick to his stomach at the thought of anything happening to the little girl, but he was working hard to maintain a professional demeanor as he went about the task of trying to find her.

"Mrs. Ward, did you recognize the man you saw going into your husband's workshop yesterday?" he asked, doing his best to draw her attention back to him.

May blinked several times, her face collapsing once more into confused furrows.

"Do you know what the man was doing on your property?" Mallory prodded.

She cocked her head to one side. "Passing through," she answered in a wistful tone. "Always passing through."

"Passing through?" Mallory echoed. "What do you mean, Mrs. Ward? There's only one road in and out of Brooksbury."

A glazed expression came over May's face as she shuffled in faded pink, fuzzy slippers back across the room to the couch and seated herself next to her husband, muttering softly.

Mallory waited until she fell silent and then tried again. "Mrs. Ward, do you remember what color the truck was that you saw parked outside?"

May turned to her husband, scraping the loose, rutted skin on her cheek with yellowing nails. "What did he say?"

Walt threw Mallory a conspiratorial glance. "I'm afraid that's the end of that conversation. She's back to her usual. You won't get anything else worth out of her today. You'll only wind her up if you keep going at it and then she'll start moaning or screaming. It won't be pretty."

Mallory gave a curt nod of acknowledgement. It was disappointing, but Walt knew his wife best. There was no sense wasting any more time here if May was unable to give them anything concrete that they could follow up on. He sensed from Ava's body language that she was eager to leave and pursue a more worthwhile lead. "If May remembers any additional details, please give me a call right away," Mallory said adjusting his holster.

"Sure will," Walt replied.

Mallory got to his feet. "You don't mind if we take a quick scout around the sheds on our way out, do you?"

"Have at it," Walt said in a genial tone. "Just make sure to bolt the doors behind you when you're done. I don't want them blowing open in the storm tonight."

Mallory turned to Ava as he pulled out his phone. "Let's go, we need to call this lead in and have someone jump on it in case there's anything to it."

THEIR SEARCH of the sheds revealed nothing untoward. At a cursory glance, Mallory could see Walt hadn't spent much time in his workshop of late, as he'd stated. Most of the tools were swathed in cobwebs and the shelves were slathered with a coating of dust so thick it heralded another era. Curiously, the only item that looked like it might have been used lately was a portable air compressor sitting just inside the door. Walt might have pulled it out to add air to a tire at some point and forgotten to put it away. On the other hand, if May was telling the truth about a stranger entering the workshop, it could have been used by him as recently as yesterday. Mallory took a quick picture of it to remind himself to send an officer out to dust for fingerprints just in case.

Back in the squad car, Mallory radioed the possible lead of a stranger sighting in the area into the station and then called Justin and Brent to update them. Without a description of either the man or the truck, there wasn't much of a line of inquiry to pursue, but it was important nonetheless to keep everyone apprised of any developments along the way. After he hung up, he turned to Ava. "The good news is that if there is a stranger driving a truck around these parts, he hasn't left the area yet. Our team has been stopping everyone at the road block. Whoever that man is who dropped by the Walt's yesterday—assuming he exists—he's still in the area."

"How are you going to find him?" Ava asked.

Mallory considered the question, trying to decide how much hope to give her in what he believed to be essentially more or less a dead end lead as it stood. "To start with, we're calling around all the residents, asking if anyone has seen an unfamiliar or out-of-town truck, or a stranger in town."

Ava smoothed a hand over her furrowed brow. "He could be hiding someplace remote. If he abducted Melanie, he might be holed up with her in a hunting cabin somewhere."

"We're covering that angle too. We have the forest service checking every campsite and hunting cabin on the map. I asked them to stay in contact with the station and give us regular updates as they work their way through the list. It's possible this guy's moving between campgrounds. In the meantime, you and I can stop by Fred Doherty's house before we head back to your place. He has a good view of both the road and the lake from his property. If he saw a truck driving away from the Wards' place at some point yesterday, he might be able to give us a description."

Ava rubbed her hands over her face, her expression grim. "That's if his eyesight's up to par. He's even older than the Wards. I'm afraid we're only going to be wasting more time chasing down dead ends when we could be out there looking for Melanie."

Mallory threw her an apologetic look. "I didn't realize May Ward had gone downhill so much. Still, we can't discount the fact that she might have given us our first real lead. I think it's worth calling on Fred to see if he might have spotted the truck too and can give us any more details."

Mallory didn't add that he was crossing his fingers. He

wasn't overly optimistic the lead would amount to anything, but for now it was all they had.

A SPRIGHTLY FRED DOHERTY was eagle-eyed and alert when Mallory and Ava knocked on his front door a few minutes later. He ushered them into a small kitchen and pulled out a couple of chairs for them before seating himself in his rocker. Mallory wasted no time bringing him up to speed on the nature of their visit.

Fred smoothed out his white mustache as he directed a look of heartfelt sympathy Ava's way. "If my dang knees weren't shot, I'd be out there helping Justin and the volunteers right now."

"I appreciate that very much, Fred," Ava said, wringing her hands and blinking back tears.

Mallory leaned forward in his chair. "We were just over at the Wards and May mentioned seeing a strange truck at her place yesterday while Walt was in town. You didn't happen to see it on the road at any point?"

Fred rested his elbows on the arms of the rocker. "Can't say I did. Course a freight train could have gone by and I wouldn't have seen or heard a thing if I was napping. You get to my age, you tend to nod off if you sit for too long." His thin lips tugged into a self-conscious smile.

"We were hoping you could confirm her story," Mallory replied. "Walt explained that May has dementia. It's possible she imagined a stranger pulling up outside, or she was remembering something that happened in the past."

Fred raised a scraggly eyebrow. "That's too bad. I heard May was going downhill. And I did notice she was a tad forgetful the last time I saw her out and about. I had an aunt with dementia back in the day and us kids were scared out of our skins around her. She'd start shrieking and boxing our ears every time she set eyes on us. Thought we were gonna rob her. Scary thing for a kid, I'll tell you."

"So you haven't seen any strangers around, out-of-season campers, a hitchhiker perhaps?" Mallory continued, steering the conversation back on track.

"No, I haven't." Fred eyed Ava with a regretful look. "And I'm real sorry to hear about your daughter going missing. I remember Gordon at her age. He was a wanderer too. Always coming over to visit my horses. Course it was different back then, wasn't it? That's what childhood was for, pottering about and exploring." He hesitated, scratching at his stubble as though something had just occurred to him. "Where is Gordon? I don't recall seeing him much in the past few months."

"I haven't either," Ava responded drily. "We're getting a divorce. He's here now of course, under the circumstances."

"Right, I see." Fred threw Mallory a pained look as he ran a hand self-consciously down the frayed sleeve of his sweater. "Well, I'll certainly keep my eyes peeled for any strangers and I can promise you I'll be on my knees tonight praying they find that little Melanie soon."

"Thanks for your time, Fred," Mallory said, slapping his thigh. "You have my number if you spot anything suspicious in the meantime."

A thick snow was beginning to fall when he and Ava stepped back outside. Mallory started up the engine and turned the car around in the driveway. "We're not going to accomplish anything more tonight other than getting stuck in a snowdrift. I'll take you back to your cabin and then I'm going home to catch a couple of hours sleep."

"Thank you, Mallory. I appreciate everything you're doing to help," Ava said, picking at her fingers. "I want to apologize for Gordon's rude behavior earlier. It's me he's angry with. He's worried about our daughter and he doesn't like to feel helpless—it brings out the worst in him."

"That's understandable," Mallory replied, twisting the knob on his scanner. He knew better than to point out that Gordon was just being Gordon and, from Mallory's perspective, the man hadn't mellowed with time. It baffled him what Ava had ever seen in him to begin with. But it was entirely possible Gordon had presented himself in a different light outside of Brooksbury. Ava hadn't known him as the troubled kid who lied to his classmates and manipulated his teachers, and she wasn't privy to the police records Mallory had access to. After Gordon had been caught swinging his neighbor's cat around by the tail and tossing it into the bushes, he'd been diagnosed with conduct disorder at the ripe old age of eight and Patricia had been forced to take him to a child psychiatrist. He'd straightened up somewhat after that, but he'd harbored a mean streak all through high school and was never someone Mallory had cared to hang out with. The incident the night of their senior prom had only aggravated the bad blood between them.

A few minutes later, they turned down Ava's lane and pulled up outside the cabin next to Gordon's black Cadillac.

"I'll keep my phone on tonight," Mallory said. "Call me if you need me or if there are any developments on your end."

Ava thanked him again and clambered out, ducking against the bracing snowstorm as she made a beeline for the cabin.

MALLORY PULLED into his garage and climbed out of his car hoping that Tammy was already asleep. It was easier not to have to feign interest in how her day had gone. No matter how hard he tried, it always led to an argument over something insignificant that had nothing to do with the real issues that had driven them apart in the first place. Deep down he knew Tammy resented the fact that his career had never gone anywhere, leaving them stuck in Brooksbury. The truth was, he was exactly where he wanted to be. He wasn't cut out for the fast-paced city life that Tammy craved. He had hoped to start a family in the low-key community they had grown up in, but Tammy had baulked at the idea after they were married, a betrayal that had driven a deep wedge between them. To add insult to injury, she'd taken the liberty of spreading the rumor that they were unable to have kids.

He pushed open the door to the mud room and hesitated when he saw that the kitchen light was still on. Steeling himself for an icy reception, he made his way along the corridor, schooling his face to a well-rehearsed neutral.

Tammy was seated at the kitchen table, staring down at her phone, her lips unconsciously tugging into a smile. She looked up, startled, when she heard Mallory enter and flicked her long, dark, silky hair over her shoulder, cappuccino eyes narrowing as she scrutinized him. "Wasn't sure I'd see you back here tonight. I heard about the Galbraith kid. How's Gordon holding up?" Her brow furrowed. "I take it he's here."

"Yeah, he arrived this afternoon. He and Ava are devastated of course. They're both in shock."

Tammy tutted and picked at her robe. "Such a sad situation. Is Gordon spending the night at the cabin?"

Mallory shrugged. "I assume so. He'll want to be there when they find Melanie."

"*If* they find her in that blizzard." Tammy stuffed her phone into her pocket and uncrossed her long legs. "Sheer negligence on her mother's part. No wonder Gordon and Ava are getting a divorce."

Mallory rubbed a hand over his jaw. "How'd you hear about that?"

"Justin's wife mentioned it when I ran into her at the market." Tammy rested her elbows on the table and interlaced her long fingers. "I'm amazed Patricia managed to keep that juicy tidbit all to herself until now. I guess her golden boy Gordon's not so golden after all."

Mallory stared at her bare fingers. He'd noticed Tammy hadn't been wearing her wedding ring of late. After a moment's reflection, he decided against bringing it up and shattering an otherwise relatively civil exchange. "What do you mean he's not so golden?"

Tammy threw him a scandalized look. "There are all sorts of rumors flying around as to why the Galbraiths are divorcing, abuse, affairs, you name it."

Mallory grunted. "Not my concern unless it relates to Melanie's disappearance."

"Any updates, leads, suspects?" Tammy arched an elongated brow. "Is this an abduction or a case of reckless child endangerment?"

Mallory poured himself a glass of water and sat down at the table opposite Tammy. "Don't know. We don't have any leads." He frowned at the glass in front of him. Technically that wasn't true, but May Ward wasn't exactly a reliable witness and he didn't want baseless rumors of a stranger abducting children getting out and frightening the residents of Brooksbury needlessly.

"Do you think Ava Galbraith could have had anything to do with her daughter's disappearance?" Tammy asked, studying him with an air of charged curiosity.

Mallory considered the question for a moment. Truth be told, he was still wrestling with that idea himself. He hadn't figured Ava out yet. He didn't really want to analyze the perplexing case any more tonight, but the fact that Tammy was making an effort to engage him in conversation for once merited some kind of response. "My gut tells me she wasn't involved but she's hiding something. I can't put my finger on it. Naturally, we're looking into her too."

"You can never rule the mother out," Tammy said, fanning out her painted fingers to stifle a yawn. "It's shocking what some mothers do to their own young."

"Let's talk about something less depressing." Mallory plastered a grin on his face. "What have you been up to this evening?" He gestured to the phone sticking out of Tammy's pocket. "Leveling up on your latest game?"

"It's either that or watching reruns of Crime Watch." Tammy gave a mirthless laugh. "What's a girl to do to kill time in a place like Brooksbury?"

Mallory gripped the glass in his hands tightly at the barbed comment. "It doesn't have to be like this, you know, Tammy. All eggshells and stilted conversation. I know we've disappointed each other, but we can get back to what we used to have."

"Therein lies the problem," Tammy retorted, a mocking undertone in her voice. "*We* never had anything."

"That's not true." Mallory shot her a pleading look. "We can move away and start over if that's what it's going to take to make you happy. I know you want a more glamorous life-style than what Brooksbury has to offer."

"I don't want to talk about us." Tammy tightened her robe around her and got to her feet. "If that's where this is going, I'm off to bed. You should probably head upstairs and get some sleep too."

Mallory took another swig of his water. The import of her words wasn't lost on him. Tammy had taken to sleeping in the downstairs guest bedroom more often than not, claiming she had a hard time falling asleep and didn't want to be disturbed by his odd hours. He could hardly criticize her for it—she was right that he was rarely around anymore and came back late most nights. But the job wasn't to blame. If he was being honest with himself, he worked the long hours to avoid going home to the same old arguments and equally draining silences while Tammy engaged in mindless games on her phone. He sighed as he placed his glass in the sink. Better a gaming addiction than a gambling one. If they were destined to follow in the Galbraith's steps all the way to the divorce court, he'd rather not be bankrupt on the front end.

9

*P*atricia flung the door to the guest room wide open, her eyes zig-zagging frantically around the space in search of her granddaughter's sleeping form. Had she fallen out of bed? She dashed around to the other side of the queen sleigh bed in a panic, but Melanie wasn't curled up on the deep pile carpet, her little chest rising and falling in sleep as it had been less than an hour earlier.

"Melanie! Where are you, honey?" she cried out, failing miserably to keep the mounting hysteria out of her voice. "Are you hiding on Gammy?" She slid open the closet door, hoping to find a wide-eyed four-year-old sitting cross-legged beneath the hems of her dresses smiling up at her. Her chest felt so tight she could barely catch a breath. Beside herself with fear, she yanked aside her out-of-season clothing, knocking over an assortment of shoeboxes in her haste. Her granddaughter was nowhere to be seen. The dull panicked beat in her chest escalated until she thought she might be having a heart attack. She leaned against the closet frame and forced herself to take several deep, calming breaths. She needed to gather her thoughts and conduct a methodical search. Melanie have must have woken up momentarily and then fallen back to sleep somewhere else in the house.

Dropping to her knees, she crawled under the bed and shoved aside the plastic tubs of spare blankets and old sheets, a thousand thoughts catapulting through her brain at once. Melanie shouldn't have woken up yet. How could the sleeping pill have worn off in less than an hour? Patricia had measured the dose meticulously and watched to make sure Melanie finished off every drop of her hot chocolate. She backed slowly out from under the bed, careful not to bump her head on the frame. Melanie had to be somewhere in the house, she might even be looking for her, or hiding on her— one of her favorite things to do.

"Mels, it's Gammy! Are you playing hide-and-seek with me?" Grunting as she got to her feet, she called out again, "Where are you sweet, baby girl?"

She exited the guest bedroom and carefully checked each of the other bedrooms and bathrooms in turn before hurrying back up the hallway to search for Melanie in the main living area of the house. Adrenalin pumping through her, she flung all the cushions off the couches and opened all the kitchen cabinet doors on the off chance Melanie had crawled into one and fallen asleep while waiting on Gammy to find her. Patricia wet her parched lips and passed a trembling hand over her brow. This couldn't be happening. There had to be a simple explanation. She berated herself for ever giving Melanie the sleeping pill. It had been unnecessary— overkill. She should have kept her granddaughter in the kitchen with her, baking or doing crafts like they often did.

Kicking back into gear, she peered into the pantry, then checked the laundry room, mudroom, and garage, even ducking under the desk in the office that adjoined the kitchen. There was no trace of Melanie anywhere. Nauseous with fear, Patricia racked her brains trying to figure out where else her granddaughter could be. Her eyes widened. Could she have gone outside to the playhouse? Without a second's hesitation, Patricia ran through the kitchen and bolted out the back door in her slippers to search for her granddaughter in the snow-covered back yard. She cupped her hands to her face to call for her, and then hesitated in the middle of her patio—Melanie wasn't supposed to be here, and neither was she for that matter. Anyone walking by with their dogs might overhear her yelling for her granddaughter. She needed to be more discreet. After a quick glance around the yard, she trudged through the snow to the playhouse and peered inside, despair threatening to overtake her senses. She ran her fingers through her hair as she scanned the deserted garden, trying to collect her thoughts. Melanie couldn't possibly be outside. She wasn't tall enough to reach the lock and open the door by herself. Patricia had made doubly sure to lock the doors at both ends of the house, as Tammy had instructed her.

With renewed hope, she retraced her steps inside, kicked off her soaked slippers, and rubbed the circulation back into her feet. She would begin searching again in the main part of the house and work her way back to the bedrooms, hunting more thoroughly this time. After all, Melanie was tiny enough to squeeze herself into the smallest of spaces.

After scouring through every closet, basket and shelf, and tearing the beds and couches apart a second time, Patricia soon found herself back in the guest bedroom where she had put Melanie to sleep earlier that morning. She hunted through the entire room again, even opening the plastic storage tubs beneath the bed and tipping the contents out on the floor on the slim chance a groggy Melanie had crawled inside one to hide and then fallen asleep again. After she'd turned the room upside down, going so far as to strip the covers from the bed, she sank down on the soft pile carpet and clapped a hand over her mouth. *No! No! No!* This wasn't supposed to be happening. This was definitely not part of the plan. It was all wrong. Where on earth could Melanie be?

She forced herself to concentrate, evaluating and eliminating the possibilities. Melanie must have woken up while she was on the phone with Tammy or folding the laundry, and found her way outside. There was no other explanation for it. Somehow she had managed to unlock the door on her own. Patricia let out a groan. Kids were always so much smarter than you gave them credit for. She had underestimated her young granddaughter. She was probably wandering around in the snow somewhere, disoriented and drowsy, dressed only in her thermal long johns. With no jacket or gloves or hat to keep her warm. Not even her boots!

Patricia hugged herself to stop from shaking, her eyes drifting to the guest bedroom window. She frowned, a niggling fear stirring in her gut. Something was amiss. The drapes looked disturbed. A sickening feeling crept steadily over her. She clambered to her feet and walked across the room to pull the heavy drapes aside. Her heart skipped a beat. The window was pulled closed, but unlatched! How was that possible? Surely Melanie couldn't have opened the window by herself. It was even farther out of her reach than the locks on the doors. Patricia peered out into the empty back yard, her eyes desperately scanning the space for a tiny figure in long johns. Stark branches waved lethargically back at her from a bleak, white winter garden. If Melanie had climbed out the window, she might have found her way out to the road by now.

Swallowing down the acid tang of fear, Patricia sprang into action, tripping her way down the hallway toward the front door. Her pulse drummed in her temples when she caught sight of Melanie's purple wool hat with the oversized pom pom hanging on the coat rack, along with a tiny jacket and snow pants, critical items reminding her just how dire the situation really was. She clapped a hand to the side of her head and moaned out loud. Her granddaughter would freeze to death in no time in this weather. She had to find her before it was too late, and she needed help to do it. Whipping out her phone, she frantically hit the redial button.

"Tammy," she gasped. "Melanie's gone. The guest bedroom window's unlatched ... I don't know how ... I thought it was ... she must have woken up and crawled outside ... I don't know what to—"

"Calm down, Patricia! Take a moment and breathe. Melanie's only four-years-old. She can't have gone far and she certainly didn't crawl out through the bedroom window. She's likely tucked in a corner of the house somewhere with her favorite stuffed animal, fast asleep."

"That's what I thought too at first," Patricia wailed. "But I've searched the house from one end to the other, twice now. And the back yard. There's no sign of her anywhere."

After a pause, Tammy asked, "Are you positive the bedroom window's unlatched?"

Patricia gulped back a hard lump in her throat. "Yes. And kids can climb, Tammy. You have no idea what they're capable of. They're like little monkeys."

"It's more likely she went out the door," Tammy said. "Was it unlocked when you went out to look for her? Maybe you forgot to lock it."

Patricia scrunched her eyes shut, trying to remember. "I ... I'm not sure. I was in such a panic I didn't pay attention."

"Okay, listen to me very carefully. She might have woken up feeling groggy and pottered outside to look for her mother. It's too cold for her to wander far. She's probably walking down your driveway or somewhere close by."

"She's not! I'm telling you she's not there." Patricia scraped her fingernails down the side of her scalp. "I can't believe this is happening. This is like some sort of Karma for what I did."

"Pull yourself together, Patricia. Go back outside and look for her again. Then call me back."

Patricia blinked back salty tears. "What if I don't find her?"

"Then I'll come over there and help you. You need to take a few deep breaths and calm down. You're going to find her. Just do an orderly search of your yard, not some panicked flyby. In the meantime, I'll turn on the police scanner in case there are any developments."

"All right, I guess. I'll call you back in a few minutes." Patricia ended the call and set her phone down on the hall table with trembling fingers.

After gearing up in her outerwear, she slipped out the front door and took off at a brisk pace down the road, eyes scanning in every direction for any trace of Melanie. In the unlikely event she ran into anyone, she would tell them that she had cut her trip to Chicago short. As she walked, she kept up a steady laser sweep of both sides of the road, searching for a tiny figure toddling along in purple leggings. A gasp escaped her lips when she realized she'd left her phone in the house. A prickling sweat broke out over her neck. Should she go back for it, or keep going? What if Tammy heard something on the scanner and tried to alert her? She needed to fetch her phone before she went any farther in case she missed an important call. After one last desperate glance down the desolate road, she wheeled around and ran the whole way back to her house. She jammed her key in the door and stumbled inside to grab her mobile from the hall table where she'd tossed it.

When she glimpsed the text from Gordon on the screen, she sucked in an icy breath.

Melanie's missing. I know who took her.

*P*atricia stared in disbelief at the text as she reread it more slowly a second time. Did Gordon know she had taken Melanie? No! He couldn't possibly. He thought she was still in Chicago with her girlfriend. Besides, he would never imagine for a minute that she would stoop to anything like this. He must have jumped to the wrong conclusion. Maybe he thought Ava had staged an abduction to blackmail him into giving her custody. There were several missed calls and voice mails from Gordon as well as the text, but Patrica couldn't bring herself to listen to any of them. She already felt guilty enough without wanting to be reminded about what this was doing to her son. She rubbed her brow distractedly, willing herself to think through things logically. She couldn't respond to Gordon's text yet. The timeline was all wrong. She needed to stay focused on the task at hand. The first priority was to get back outside and find Melanie, just like Tammy said. That would make everything all right again. She could revert to her original plan and still call Mallory later on to make her report.

Patricia stuffed her phone into her pocket and pulled the

front door shut behind her as she set out once more to search for Melanie. Blizzard conditions were predicted overnight. She needed to find her granddaughter before it started snowing hard. No part of her plan had included exposing her precious Melanie to the elements, especially not dressed as she was. She doggedly trudged up and down the road for half a mile in both directions, and then began walking around the perimeter of the fields that bordered the road on the off chance that a disoriented Melanie had crawled under a hedgerow and fallen asleep again.

After searching for the best part of an hour, Patricia dug out her phone and called Tammy back, frantic with fear. "I can't find her anywhere. Should I drive past Gordon's cabin and make sure she's not there? Someone might have picked her up by now. Maybe I should check if the emergency vehicles are still parked outside. I just don't know what—"

"They haven't found her yet," Tammy confirmed. "I've been listening to the scanners the entire time. Get back inside your house before someone sees you. I'm coming over."

Tammy ended the call abruptly. Patricia's fingers shook so hard the phone slipped from her hand. She bent down and picked it up, brushing the snow from the case. What in the world had she done? She should never have listened to Tammy Anderson and her madcap idea to begin with. The girl had always been trouble. Devious and manipulative. If anything happened to Melanie, Patricia would never forgive herself for conspiring with such a dangerous ally to pull off this stunt.

Back in her house, she went straight to the drinks cabinet and poured herself a generous shot of brandy. She set the crystal tumbler down on the island and stared dully around her gleaming white kitchen where Melanie had spent endless hours decorating cookies, chattering happily about her preschool friends, and coloring pictures of fairies—her current career choice for when she was *all growed up*. Patricia felt sick to her stomach as Melanie's squeaky voice seemed to echo from every corner of the room in condemnation of what she had set in motion. Ordinarily, it brought Patricia immense pleasure to admire her gourmet kitchen's clean lines, but the clinical space now appeared as stark and silent as a morgue. She reached for her glass and downed the shot in one gulp, willing it to numb the pain that was spreading through her insides like a fast-growing cancer.

An insistent knocking on the back door shocked her out of her grim musings. She stood frozen to the spot half-expecting Mallory's booming voice to shout, "Police! Open up!"

A moment later, Patricia's phone pinged with a text from Tammy.

Let me in! I'm at the back door.

She forced her leaden legs to move across the kitchen floor to let Tammy in. The minute she opened the door, Tammy took charge, and Patricia wilted in her wake, gratefully following her lead—after all, she reasoned, Tammy was married to a police officer, she must know what to do in these kinds of circumstances. Patricia, on the other hand, was not in any way prepared for the awful scenario that had unfolded.

"Now, we're going to repeat some of the steps you've taken so bear with me," Tammy began. "It's possible in your panicked state you overlooked a hiding spot. We'll search the house together this time. Two sets of eyes are better than one."

Patricia gave a despondent nod, resigning herself to the hopeless task as she fell into step with Tammy. Painstakingly, they combed every inch of the house, including the basement and attic, and then walked the deserted road several hundred feet in both directions without finding any footprints or any other trace of Melanie.

"I walked around the hedgerows already," Patricia said. "I'm telling you she's not here, Tammy. She's disappeared into thin air."

"All right, I'll take my car and drive around for a bit. Maybe she got farther than we realized."

"It's no use," Patricia moaned. "I have to call Gordon. He's bound to be wondering why I haven't responded to his text or any of his calls."

"Don't be ridiculous." Tammy threw her an alarmed look. "What are you going to tell him? That you kidnapped his child and lost her a couple of hours later? This is supposed to be about Ava being a negligent parent, not his mother abducting his child."

"I know, I know, but it's all gone terribly wrong. I just don't know what else to do." Patricia squeezed her face between her hands. "I can't risk leaving Melanie out in a blizzard all night."

Tammy let out a sympathetic sigh. "Patricia, darling, the police and SAR are already out there looking for her. Calling up Mallory and telling him what you did won't accomplish anything other than getting yourself arrested."

Patricia turned and stared at Tammy in horror. "He can't do that. I'm Melanie's grandmother. I'm family."

Tammy pulled her lips together in a disapproving line. "In the eyes of the law, you're also her abductor. That's how they're going to view this. Now, listen up and let me help you. The first thing you need to do is hide Melanie's outerwear, including that ridiculous pom pom hat hanging on your coat rack that's in the photo on the missing flyers being handed out."

"But, you said—"

"—to call Mallory this afternoon and let him know you

came back from Chicago early and that I found Melanie wandering unsupervised at the lake, half frozen, and brought her straight to your house. We're sticking to the plan. You can't fall apart on me now." Tammy snatched Melanie's clothes from the rack and reached for her furry snow boots lined up on the tile below. "I'll get rid of these for you."

Patricia ran her fingers through her silver bob. She was hyper-ventilating and could barely think straight, but it was becoming increasingly clear that she needed to take back control from Tammy before the situation became any more convoluted. What she was proposing now—hiding evidence —was unarguably criminal. It would only make everything worse in the long run. "But Gordon will know what to do," she protested. "I have to tell him what's happened to his daughter."

"You can't say anything to anyone." Tammy gripped her arm, her eyes flashing a dangerous brew of emotions. "If you do, you will be prosecuted and you *will* go to prison, Patricia. Do you understand what I'm telling you?"

She let out a despairing sob. "I just need them to find her."

"And they will," Tammy said, relaxing her grip. "Trust me, they will find her. And this will all end the way we planned it, with Ava being declared an unfit mother. Now, let me take a quick drive around and see if I can spot her."

Patricia reached for the front door knob, but Tammy laid a hand on her arm. "I'll go out through the garage. I can't risk anyone seeing me with an armful of Melanie's clothes."

After Tammy left, Patricia paced inside her house for the next couple of hours, waiting in vain for a call or a text letting her know that Tammy had found Melanie safe and sound. The only comfort she could draw from all of this was knowing that a team of professionals was out there looking for her granddaughter. But guilt and fear were eating her alive. As darkness closed in, and the wind whipped into a frenzy, Patricia wrestled with her decision before finally breaking down in tears and reaching for her phone. It was time to come clean with Gordon. But she couldn't bring herself to tell him in a lousy text what she had done. Instead, she let him know that she'd arrived back from Chicago early to beat the storm and was having a panic attack over the news about Melanie.

When Gordon rang her doorbell a half hour later, she cast a furtive look up and down the street before ushering him in and closing the door behind him.

They held each other in the hallway for several minutes without saying a word. Tears streamed silently down Patricia's face as the magnitude of what she had conspired to do hit her. When they broke apart, she pulled a tissue from her sleeve and wiped her eyes. "I'm so sorry, Gordon."

He let out a snort of disgust. "I should have expected something like this. It's exactly the kind of stunt she would pull."

Patricia took a thready breath and fixed a questioning look on her son. "Who are you talking about?"

"Ava! Who else?" He stomped down the hallway and disappeared into the kitchen. Patricia followed him and pulled out a leather bar stool from the island while he grabbed a beer from the fridge. He sat down next to her and stared morosely at the black and gray swirls in the gleaming white slab of granite he had helped pick out and pay for. Patricia bit her trembling bottom lip. Gordon really was a good son, and up until now she had considered herself to be a good mother and grandmother. What she had done today was unforgivable.

"I don't know what Ava's game is," Gordon growled. "But I suspect it's about money. She's not happy with what she'll get in the divorce thanks to the prenup." He put the beer bottle to his lips and chugged down a good quarter of its contents. "She knows where Melanie is. I can tell by her body language. She's acting the part of the distraught mother, but there's no real fear in her eyes. She wants me to sweat it out though, and she wants me and forty odd SAR volunteers to believe Melanie is lost in the snow somewhere by the lake."

Patricia sucked in a silent breath. This was not good at all. If Gordon believed Melanie was safe and that Ava was hiding her somewhere, he wouldn't put enough pressure on the police to find her. Patricia couldn't allow that to happen. Melanie was in real danger of succumbing to the elements. She had no choice but to tell him everything. She had done it for him, surely he would understand that she hadn't meant for it all to go so horribly awry. She'd only wanted to teach Ava a lesson, to give her the kind of scare she deserved for what she was doing to Gordon.

Patricia had felt powerless when Gordon first broke the news to her that Ava had filed for divorce. When she'd found out that Ava wanted full custody, a righteous anger had quickly replaced her feelings of powerlessness. She'd resolved then and there to find a way to make sure Ava wouldn't get to keep her granddaughter from her. Knowing she would find a sympathetic ear in Tammy, she had complained bitterly about the situation to her at a community fundraiser. It was Tammy who had come up with the *Gammy snatch* as she'd laughingly called it at the time. "You just need to keep Melanie hidden long enough to make Ava sweat and raise some red flags about her competence as a mother," Tammy had suggested. "Custody will be a slam dunk after that."

At first Patricia hadn't been able to figure out how to pull it off. But when Gordon mentioned to her that Ava and Melanie were coming up to the cabin without him to clean out Ava's stuff, she'd recognized an opportunity. She had quietly changed her return ticket and arrived home from

Chicago late Wednesday night without informing anyone other than Tammy, who swiftly put together a plan. Taking Melanie had seemed like the right thing to do at the time. A corrective measure to counteract Ava's manipulative bid to gain custody. Two could play at that game. Besides, Ava really was an irresponsible mother, always easily distracted. She'd been so engrossed in her photography that she hadn't even noticed her four-year-old daughter had wandered off. She absolutely didn't deserve Melanie.

But, Patricia never in her wildest dreams imagined the whole plan would backfire like this. Hopefully, her part in it wasn't illegal—she knew Gordon wouldn't press charges against her, but what about Ava? Patricia wrinkled her forehead in concentration. She could frame it in such a way as to make Tammy responsible, it had all been her idea, after all, and Tammy had carried out the actual abduction. Her stomach roiled with fear as she laid a manicured hand on her son's arm.

"Gordon, darling, there's something I need to tell you."

He took another swig of beer and grunted. "If it's about Ava, I don't want to hear it. I'm sick to death of that wretched woman and everything she's done to make my life difficult."

"It's not about Ava, it's about Tammy Anderson."

PATRICIA ROSE QUIETLY and went into the utility room to fetch a broom and dustpan to sweep up the broken pieces of glass from the bottle Gordon had thrown at the wall. As she'd expected, he had exploded when she told him what she'd done, but his rage hadn't been vented at her. As soon as she'd mentioned Tammy's involvement, his whole demeanor had changed. That's when he'd thrown the bottle and smashed his fist into the kitchen door. And, when he'd calmed down enough to catch his breath, he'd dropped his own bombshell. "Tammy and I have been seeing each other on and off since high school. I didn't tell you because I knew how you felt about her. I finally broke it off for good a couple of weeks ago and she didn't take it well."

Patricia's mouth fell open as the room spun around her. Pieces slowly began to fall into place. Tammy's eagerness to side with her against Ava, the plot to abduct her own granddaughter. Of course! Tammy had wanted to be integral to helping Gordon gain custody in the hope she could win him back.

"So I was wrong about Ava staging this stunt," Gordon fumed. "It was Tammy all along. I get it now and it makes perfect sense." A dangerous edge crept into his voice. "She set this whole thing up to get back at me for breaking it off with her. She has Melanie."

Patricia shook her head in disbelief. "No, you've got it all wrong. Tammy brought Melanie here. She was only trying to help you win custody."

Gordon let out a snort of disgust. "It goes way beyond that. She duped you, Mother. She preyed on your fear that you might not see your granddaughter again after the divorce, she used you to gain access to Melanie. She brought her here, but then she had her abducted from your house. This has nothing to do with you, or Ava, or even custody of Melanie. This is all about Tammy punishing me for ending our relationship."

Patricia wet her lips, trying to digest what Gordon was saying. Could it be true? Had Tammy used her for a more sinister purpose? It dawned on her that Tammy had had ample opportunity to unlatch the window in the guest bedroom while Patricia warmed the milk for Melanie's hot chocolate. Her heartbeat clattered in her chest. But, this was a good thing, wasn't it? It meant she hadn't lost Melanie after all. If Tammy had taken her to get back at Gordon, they could end this nightmare now. She reached for her phone lying on the granite counter. "I'll call Mallory right away and let him know what his wife has done so he can arrest her."

Gordon grabbed her wrist. "No! Wait a minute! Let's think this through first. If you call Mallory, he'll find out about the affair and everything will blow up. Let me handle this directly with Tammy and find out what she wants from me first. Maybe we can get Melanie back ourselves and avoid involving the police any further."

Without waiting for Patricia's response, he pulled out his phone and tapped on a contact before hitting the speaker button. "The game's up, Tammy. Mother told me everything. I want my daughter back."

On the other end of the line, Tammy let out a callous rip of laughter. "Naughty Patricia! She just doesn't listen very well which is aggravating. What kind of a tall tale did she tell you, darling?"

Patricia gasped and clapped a hand to her mouth.

Gordon began to pace. "I know you have Melanie and I need you to—"

"What you *need*, Gordon, is a wake-up call! You're a rotten father who's never there for his child. You're no better than Ava in that department. Neither of you should have custody of that child."

"Tammy, I'm warning you. This has gone far enough. She's only four-years-old and—"

"I don't have her so don't bother groveling," Tammy snapped. "And don't even think about turning up on my doorstep because I'll tell Mallory you've been stalking me, or worse. And we both know the chain of sordid secrets that would come to light if he investigates those charges."

"You're a sociopath, you know that don't you, Tammy? Only a—"

The call disconnected. Gordon swore softly and hit redial, but Tammy didn't pick up.

Patricia pressed her manicured hands to her cheeks. "You can't let her get away with this. I'll go with you to the station and back you up. Mallory won't let her get away with this either. He's a good man."

Gordon folded his arms across his chest and glowered at her. "You don't understand. That woman is capable of destroying me. She's entangled in my world in ways that threaten to unravel everything I've worked for. I need to think this through before I make any sudden moves that could jeopardize Melanie's safety."

A shiver ran up Patricia's spine. Something about Gordon's tone made her think there was more to this abduction than met the eye. She gritted her teeth. Whatever Tammy Anderson was holding over her son's head, it was not something he wanted Mallory to get wind of, and that could only mean he was in some kind of trouble.

11

*M*allory woke to the beeping of a text coming through on his phone. Eyes at half-mast, he scrabbled around on the dresser table until his fingers latched onto his mobile. Stifling a yawn, he glanced at the screen.

Ava Galbraith received a ransom note.

He bolted out of bed, reaching for his clothes slung over a chair as he reread the text. He struggled to make sense of it while simultaneously embracing a feeling of relief that Ava's missing four-year-old daughter hadn't been lost out in the blizzard that had raged all night after all. He yanked out a drawer and rummaged around for some clean underwear. A ransom demand was not a development he had anticipated. His best analysis of Melanie's baffling disappearance so far had been to surmise that one or other of her parents had abducted her ahead of what was likely to be a contentious custody battle. His instincts were usually right about people, and both Ava and Gordon gave him the impression they were hiding secrets from him, and from each other.

His thoughts raced in several different directions at once

as he pulled a long-sleeved undershirt over his head. The ransom note changed everything. Parents fighting over money normally took it out on each other in the courts, not in ransom demands for which they could potentially face serious charges. It appeared there could be a third party involved. Whoever had abducted Melanie must know that her parents were well-heeled. The chances of a stranger stumbling upon a child in the early hours at the lake and deciding to kidnap her for ransom were slim to none. This was a carefully executed plan by someone who knew Ava's early morning routine, someone with prior knowledge that she and Melanie were going to be at the lake for the weekend. But Ava had clearly stated that she'd told no one she was coming up here. That is no one other than Gordon.

Mallory called Brent and put him on speaker as he buttoned up his flannel shirt. "FBI notified?"

"Yeah, they got a hostage negotiator on standby. Can't get up here yet with the weather how it is. The nearest airports are all closed. It could be Sunday before we see them. We're on our own until then."

Mallory rubbed a hand over his face. "Okay, break it down for me.

"The ransom note was tucked beneath Ava's windshield wiper in a padded plastic envelope," Brent explained. "Along with a Polaroid of Melanie. Ava Galbraith confirmed that her daughter's wearing the clothes she disappeared in, minus her outerwear. We sent the picture to the lab to verify it."

"Get forensics on any possible prints. I'm on my way."

THANKFULLY THE SNOW plow had already made its way down the main road, so despite the heavy snowfall overnight, Mallory managed to pull into Ava's driveway twenty-five minutes later. Brent met him outside on the front porch, a suitably somber look on his face. The Brooksbury sheriff's department had never handled a kidnapping-for-ransom case before. In theory, they knew what to do, but a young child's life was at stake and any wrong moves could prove disastrous.

"Was it a handwritten note?" Mallory asked, brows raised in hopeful expectation.

Brent shook his head. "Printed."

Mallory nodded distractedly. He'd expected as much. If this was the work of someone who knew the Galbraiths, they would have gone to great lengths to cover their tracks—maybe even to the extent of using someone else's computer and printer to write the ransom note. Mallory was still unwilling to rule out the possibility that the whole abduction had been staged as part of a custody battle. Gordon was the obvious suspect as far as Mallory was concerned, but he didn't have an obvious motive. Judging by the brand new Cadillac he drove, and the designer suits he strutted around in, the man wasn't strapped for cash. However, Mallory had learned that appearances could be deceptive, and with an expensive divorce and custody battle looming on the horizon, there was a chance this ransom request had something to do with it. "Get me the breakdown on the Galbraiths' finances," he muttered to Brent as he pushed open the front door to the cabin. "Neither of them have been ruled out as suspects yet."

Ava stood when Mallory entered the room. Her tear-streaked face was flushed. "At least we know she's alive ... we can get her back ... I'll get the money, somehow, of course," she babbled.

Mallory nodded, trying to analyze why his instincts were on high alert. Despite Ava's tears, something about her expression was off. Was he imagining it or did she look almost smug? Maybe she was close to having a breakdown, which wouldn't be unusual given the stressful circumstances. After all, this was the first indication they'd had in twenty-four hours that Melanie was still alive. If Ava was that fragile, he needed to proceed with caution and not burst her bubble of hope. They had a long road ahead of them to get Melanie back unharmed with the limited resources at their immediate disposal. "It is good news," he agreed cautiously. "A breakthrough of sorts. At least we have a direction to go in now."

"Not just a direction, a roadmap. We'll do exactly what the ransom note says," Ava said. "We can't take any chances with Melanie's life."

Mallory followed her gaze to the counter where a plastic bag and a white padded envelope lay next to a single sheet of paper. He walked over to it, pulling on a pair of gloves, and gingerly picked up the note.

If you want to see your daughter again, put $500,000 in a black duffel bag and take it to the Buttercup Campground tomorrow evening. Leave your cabin unaccompanied at precisely 6.00pm. Park your car at the turnoff from the main road about a mile away and come alone on foot. Place the bag inside the fire ring at campsite 4D. Leave immediately. Once the money has been verified, you will receive the coordinates where your daughter will be waiting for you, unharmed. If you deviate from these instructions in any way she will rest with the angels.

Mallory grimaced as he reread the last line. Only a sick, twisted human being could write something like this, threatening the life of an innocent four-year-old. Ava couldn't be behind this. Surely not even Gordon would sink to such depths when it came to talking about his daughter. This was a threat they needed to take seriously. Mallory laid the note back on the counter and examined the packaging next to it. "Who found this?"

"I did, sir," Brent replied. "SAR was forced to call off the search around midnight and Justin asked me for an update on conditions early this morning. I was walking the property when I spotted the envelope on Ava's windscreen."

Mallory frowned. "Was it covered in snow?"

"Yes, sir. Someone must have braved the blizzard to drop it off during the course of the night. It had been there for several hours at least. There were a good couple of inches of snow built up over it. Any footprints were also covered up of course."

"It doesn't matter who left it, or when," Ava piped up. "I'll do whatever these people want. I just want to get Melanie back safely. Gordon and I will get the money together somehow."

Mallory ran a hand over the back of his neck as he cast a curious glance around the room. "Where is Gordon?"

"He went to his mother's place last night after I returned," Ava said. "He found out she'd cut her trip to Chicago short and came back early. Supposedly, she was very distressed about Melanie and having difficulty breathing. Gordon was worried about her. He's coming back over here this morning."

Mallory kept his expression neutral. He wasn't really surprised to hear that Gordon was more concerned about his mother's panic attack than his wife's wellbeing, considering that he and Ava were on the verge of a nasty divorce. But it did raise the possibility that Gordon could have planted the note. He threw Brent a questioning look. "Did you tell Gordon Galbraith about the ransom note?"

"Not yet, sir."

"Good, keep it that way. I want to observe his reaction firsthand when he gets here."

Ava brushed a shaking hand over her forehead. "You don't think Gordon could possibly be behind this, do you? I mean I know he can be a jerk at times, but I can't imagine he would ever do anything to endanger Melanie, or frighten her like this."

"I'm not going to speculate on what anyone's capable of. It's my job to investigate every possible angle," Mallory replied, glancing toward the window at the sound of a vehicle pulling up outside.

Brent peered through the window. "It's the postal truck."

"Oh, yeah, I asked Jim White to stop by on his way to work," Mallory said. "Don't mention anything about the ransom note. We can't let that get out to the press. I don't want to risk scaring off Melanie's abductor before we make contact." He strode to the door and opened it. "Morning, Jim. Come on in."

The postman stepped over the threshold and glanced apprehensively around the room. When he spotted Ava, he removed his fur-lined cap and pulled down the corners of his lips. "I'm very sorry to hear about your daughter, ma'am."

Ava inclined her head and muttered her thanks, although Mallory guessed by her woebegone expression that the postman's condolences did little to comfort her. Well-meant platitudes couldn't alleviate the terror she was living through. They'd all rather hear that Jim had found Melanie wandering in the snow, that she was safe and warm in his postal truck, and that this nightmare was over. But, as the ransom note had made clear, it was only just beginning. Someone had taken a four-year-old child and was holding her hostage, demanding money for her life. This wasn't how a typical week in Brooksbury was supposed to unfold.

"Thanks for stopping by, Jim," Mallory began, "we're still trying to establish exactly what happened to Melanie. Did you happen to notice any strange vehicles in the vicinity of the lake while you were driving your route yesterday?"

"Can't say I did. There weren't many cars on the road at

all yesterday. Most folks had hunkered down ahead of the storm."

"What about the day before?"

Jim blinked a couple of times, mulling it over in his head. "I passed Sam McGregor heading into town, and the Devines. I remember waving at a few other folks too. No strangers or out-of-town vehicles that I recall. My route's a rural one though, not too busy at the best of times."

"Did you talk to anyone on your route?"

Jim scratched his scalp. "Well, let's see, old Fred Doherty was coming down the lane from his place so I pulled alongside him and handed him his mail. He was in a hurry, off to a doctor's appointment. His back's been bothering him again. After that, I stopped by the Wards and chatted to May for a few minutes. Walt had gone into town. She gets kinda lonely on her own. You know, with the dementia and all."

Mallory gave a dismissive nod, unwilling to get sidetracked by the ailments of the elderly on Jim's route. "Did you pass any strangers on foot? Hitchhikers, or campers?"

Jim frowned and shook his head. "No, no one. Too cold this time of the year. May did mention that her son had stopped by earlier that morning, but—"

"Jeremy Ward?" Mallory asked, fighting to keep his tone even.

"Yeah, I guess he must be back from Alaska, or maybe—" Jim's voice trailed off and he stared uncomfortably at Mallory.

Mallory turned to Brent. "Put an alert out. If Jeremy Ward's back in town, I want him brought in for questioning."

Jim blinked, clearly ill-at-ease. "You don't think he could have—"

"You've been extremely helpful, Jim," Mallory interrupted. "I'll take it from here."

The postman fiddled with the fur hat in his hands. "Well, if that's all you need from me, I'd best get off to work."

Mallory nodded. "Keep your radar on while you do your rounds today. Call me if you come across anything remotely suspicious or out of the ordinary, no matter how insignificant—and especially if you bump into Jeremy Ward."

"Will do." Jim pulled his cap back on, buttoned up his jacket and, with a final cursory nod to the room, made his exit.

Mallory settled his gaze on Ava. "Do you know the Wards' son, Jeremy?"

Ava blinked and pulled her brows into a befuddled frown. "No, I've never met him. Do you … think he had something to do with Melanie's disappearance?"

Mallory scrubbed a hand over his stubble, weighing his next words. He'd put money on a bet that Ava was lying to him about not knowing Jeremy Ward, but he couldn't figure out what her motive was. "Jeremy is May and Walt's only child," he said. "He served time for racketeering and a botched heist years ago. He was only nineteen when he went to prison. He wouldn't give up any of the other players in the ring, or who the mastermind was, but he was linked to some pretty heavy stuff—drugs, trafficking, money laundering, that kind of thing. The police chief at the time figured Jeremy must have been paid handsomely to keep his mouth shut. He moved to Alaska when he got out of prison. As far as I know, he hasn't been back to Brooksbury since. He knew he wasn't welcome around these parts anymore."

Ava's expression remained studiously blank. "Do you think it could have been Jeremy's truck that May saw?"

"It's anyone's guess. May gets confused easily. She could have been remembering Jeremy pulling up twenty years ago for all I know." Mallory grimaced when he recalled the air compressor sitting on the floor behind Walt's workshop door. Someone had used it recently. He needed to find out if they'd got any prints on it yet. He studied the ransom note lying on the kitchen counter. Five-hundred-thousand dollars was considerably more money than Jeremy Ward had ever made racketeering as a teenager. If he was back in town, he was definitely a person of interest.

12

*A*nother vehicle scraped to a halt in the snow that had accumulated outside Ava's cabin overnight. Moments later, Gordon and his mother, Patricia, walked past the kitchen window and made their way to the front porch.

Mallory opened the door to them and ran a practiced eye over their disheveled appearance as he greeted them. The ordinarily well-coiffed Patricia was dressed in lycra pants, snow boots and an oversized sweater and her eyes were red from crying. The last time he'd bumped into her in a restaurant a few weeks ago, she'd been turned out in knee-high fur boots and a cashmere cardigan and barely condescended to acknowledge him with an unsmiling nod as she walked by, her Louis Vuitton purse dangling from the crook of her arm. For his part, Gordon looked as if he'd slept in his expensive suit. Unshaven and pale, his eyes shifted restlessly between Mallory and Ava as he strode inside. "Where's Justin?" he demanded. "I don't see any vehicles parked outside. Why isn't SAR out there looking for my daughter?"

"Fresh volunteers are on their way," Mallory replied, making no attempt to curb the disapproval in his voice.

"They worked up until midnight in extreme conditions before calling it a night."

Patricia let out a plaintive sob, her legs wobbling beneath her.

Ava got to her feet and took a hesitant step toward her mother-in-law.

"Don't you dare come near me!" Patricia hissed in a tone of utter disdain. Gordon scowled at Ava and reached out an arm to steady his mother. She sniffed and rummaged around in her purse for a tissue. "It's your fault my granddaughter's missing in the first place. If you'd been watching her like a mother should, none of this would have happened."

Gordon shot her a warning glance and she quietened down.

She dabbed at her eyes and turned to Mallory. "Do you have any leads yet?"

"We're still in the process of contacting everyone who lives in and around Brooksbury," he responded, trying to keep his tone unruffled. Patricia Galbraith appeared to be dangerously close to having a nervous breakdown, and he already had enough to deal with without adding Gordon's hysterical mother to the roster. "In the meantime, we have a new development as of this morning."

Gordon narrowed his eyes, tugging on the cuff of his jacket. "What kind of development?"

Mallory rubbed his jaw, his eyes never leaving Gordon's face. "Someone left a ransom note on the windscreen of Ava's car last night."

Gordon blinked, momentarily stunned into silence. Mallory noted with interest the incredulous look he shot his mother before demanding, "Where is this note?"

Brent stepped forward and gestured to the counter. "You're welcome to read it but please don't touch anything. We'll need to swab it for prints."

Mallory silently observed Gordon's and Patricia's body language as they stood side-by-side reading the ransom note. Gordon clenched and unclenched his fists and then swore loudly before exchanging another loaded look from beneath his brows with his mother. Mallory found their reaction puzzling, to say the least. They both appeared to be genuinely shocked at the news about the ransom note, which at first glance seemed to indicate neither of them was behind it, but they had yet to express any relief that Melanie was alive, which Mallory also found odd and troubling. He had the strangest feeling they knew more about the note than they were letting on, maybe even who had sent it.

"Half a million dollars! What kind of a game is this sicko playing?" Gordon thumped a fist on the counter. "If you small-town cops had got your act together in a timely manner and found my daughter, it need never have come to this!"

Brent discreetly slid the ransom note out of range of any further outbursts.

"Any idea who might be behind it?" Mallory asked, directing his question at both Gordon and his mother.

Patricia averted her gaze, her face paling, her manicured fingers latching onto the edge of the counter in a death grip.

"Isn't that your job to figure out?" Gordon snapped, rubbing the back of his neck. "Now what are we supposed to do?"

"What do you mean? We're going to give them the money, Gordon!" Ava interrupted. "We're going to do whatever it takes to get our daughter back!"

"You mean *I'm* going to give them the money." Gordon scowled at her. "But conveniently, the note was left on *your* car."

"What's that supposed to mean?" Ava cried.

"It means I'm supposed to fork over half a million dollars to you and trust you to deliver it to some unknown entity."

Patricia squeezed her son's arm. "You should take the money to the campsite, Gordon. It doesn't specify which parent has to go."

"No!" Ava protested. "The note was left on my car for a reason. We're going to do exactly what it says. I won't risk Melanie's life."

"You've already done a good job of that!" Patricia spat out with venom.

"Ava's right," Mallory cut in. "We can't deviate from the ransom instructions without risking endangering Melanie further." He pinned a gaze on Gordon. "Can you get that kind of cash together at short notice?"

"I'll figure it out." Gordon folded his arms across his chest. "But I'm not comfortable handing the money over to Ava to deliver. She's already managed to lose our daughter, what if she loses the money too and we end up with nothing?" He jerked his chin in the direction of the ransom note. "This whole thing could be a set up for all we know, someone who heard Melanie's missing and is trying to pull a fast one on us. How do we even know they have Melanie?"

"They included a Polaroid of her in the envelope," Brent hastened to explain. "We sent that off to the lab to verify its authenticity."

Gordon threw him a scathing look. "If all we have is a photo, we don't know for sure if she's still alive. You need to do better than that if you expect me to agree to dump that kind of money at a campsite in the middle of nowhere."

"We haven't been given much time to verify anything, or any way of contacting the kidnapper," Mallory pointed out. He cleared his throat before continuing. "We don't have to do it this way. There are other options."

"I'm not risking involving the police and scaring off

whoever took Melanie," Ava said emphatically. "They threatened her life if we don't comply. We're going to do precisely what the note says."

Gordon moved his jaw side to side, eyes flashing with anger as he pinned his gaze on Mallory. "I agree that getting my daughter back unharmed is the top priority. But as soon as Melanie's safe, I expect you to hunt down whoever's behind this and recover every last dollar of my money."

Mallory gave a grim nod. "Believe me, we have no intention of leaving a kidnapper at large."

"I'll call my bank now and make arrangements to withdraw the cash." Gordon turned to his mother and laid a hand on her shoulder steering her toward the door. "I'll drop you home on my way."

"You'll need to bring the money down to the station so we can mark the bills before the transfer takes place," Mallory added. "Do you want a police escort?"

Gordon directed a wary look at Mallory. "No, that won't be necessary."

Mallory watched Gordon and his mother exit the cabin, mulling over what it could possibly be that they were keeping from him. Did they know who was behind the ransom note? Or did Gordon believe Ava had staged the abduction in a reckless attempt to get her hands on more of his money? Mallory frowned down at the cryptic message laying on the counter.

... she will rest with the angels.

His gut told him that neither of Melanie's parents could have written those words. It was the work of a sociopath. No one with a heart could threaten their four-year-old child that way. He grimaced. The more the case evolved, the clearer it became that they were dealing with a very disturbed individual—perhaps, more than one.

Moments after Gordon and Patricia had driven away

from the cabin, there was another knock on the front door, and Justin stuck his head inside. "We're about to resume the search. Any new information we should know about?"

Mallory walked over to the door and conversed in hushed tones with him for several minutes. When Justin closed the door behind him, Mallory turned to Ava. "I briefed Justin about the ransom note. He'll make sure the volunteers keep it confidential so the press don't get wind of it and botch up the ransom drop. Now that we know what we're dealing with, it's important the SAR volunteers focus their search on any possible hiding places in the vicinity where a kidnapper could stake out with a victim; disused sheds, abandoned buildings, barns etc. In the meantime, you need to prepare yourself for the very real possibility that you're going to end up taking that cash to the Buttercup Campground this evening." He scratched the stubble on his jaw, choosing his next words carefully. "You need to understand that it's not without risk. We have no idea who we're negotiating with at this point, or how many of them there are, but we need to assume they're armed. You'll have to wear a bulletproof vest under your jacket."

Ava swallowed hard and gave a timid nod. "I understand," she said in a wavering tone. "It's not a problem. I'm willing to do anything to get Melanie back safely."

"Sir! Text message from the station," Brent said, an undertone of urgency in his voice as he motioned Mallory over. Without a word, he handed him his phone.

Jeremy Ward's prints on air compressor. No longer resides at last known address in Alaska.

13

*P*atricia and Gordon drove the short distance from the cabin to Patricia's house in near silence. The ransom note was a twist neither of them had seen coming. Evidently Tammy Anderson had much more in mind than they had originally thought possible. Patricia couldn't stop going over in her head how duplicitous Tammy had been in plotting everything down to the last detail, and how cunningly she had used her as a point of entry to get her claws into Gordon's heart and rip it out. She cursed her own stupidity for ever believing that Tammy had cared one iota about helping her bring about Ava's downfall. She had sounded so heartfelt, so convincing in making Patricia think the *Gammy snatch* was a stroke of brilliance. But Tammy had never harbored any real interest in teaching Ava a lesson—it was enough for her to know that Gordon despised his wife. Tammy had a much more insidious agenda in mind all along. She had set out to punish Gordon for leaving her by toying with the one person he truly loved, and now it seemed she intended to relieve him of a hefty share of his money too before she turned Melanie over to him. Patricia scrunched her eyes shut and exhaled a shallow breath. Tammy's brazen scheme would never work. Gordon was cleverer than that scheming piece of trailer trash. He would figure something out. He always did.

Gordon pulled up outside the garage and rammed the shifter into park. He turned off the engine and stared straight ahead, one hand still locked around the wheel.

Patricia rubbed his arm gently. "I'm so sorry, Gordon. I never dreamed anything like this would happen."

He gave an exasperated shake of his head. "I don't blame you. She played us both. But, she won't get away with it. She's gone too far with the ransom note. It's a dangerous game to play and she's way out of her league at this point."

Patricia glanced at her watch. "The bank doesn't open for another thirty minutes. Do you want to come in for a coffee or something? I can scramble some eggs or make you an omelette."

Gordon pulled the keys from the ignition. "I'll come in for a bit. I need to make a call before I head over to the bank anyway." He unplugged his phone from the charger before climbing out of the car.

Patricia unlocked her front door and led him through to the kitchen. Her stomach twisted as she pictured Melanie sitting coloring at the counter, knees tucked beneath her on a bar stool, cupid lips parted in concentration. Her high-pitched voice echoed through the desolate chambers of Patricia's heart and she pressed her lips tightly together to cut off the cry that threatened to escape. She had to hold it together for a little longer. Gordon would fix this like he fixed everything.

"Just coffee for me, I'm not that hungry," he said, as he sat down at the island. He scrolled through his contacts and tapped on a number, bouncing his knee up and down impatiently as he waited on someone to pick up.

Patricia busied herself with the coffee, all the while listening attentively to the one-sided conversation.

"Yeah, it's me. I need you to wire five-hundred-thousand dollars to my business account right away. Got a crayon? Jot this down."

Patricia lifted two fine bone china mugs down from a wrought iron rack and set out sugar and cream while she waited for her coffeemaker to brew. Gordon had bought her one of those newfangled Nespresso machines last Christmas but she had yet to take it out of the box. The brewing process was a part of the ritual she rather enjoyed. Life was too rushed as it was without sacrificing time-honored daily ceremonies to the press of a button. She frowned to herself as Gordon recited his account number to the person on the other end of the line. If the bank wasn't open yet, who was he talking to? And didn't they need his routing number as well as his account number? Patricia felt a vague sense of unease but she wasn't exactly sure why. Gordon knew a whole lot more about these kinds of things than she did. He took care of all her financial affairs for her, as his father had before him, and she'd never encountered an issue yet. Still, she couldn't help thinking it should be a tad more difficult to come up with half a million dollars on the fly.

"Figure it out, you know the drill," Gordon said, a ring of irritation in his voice. "I'm neck high in something big right now and I can't deal with anything else until I've taken care of it."

Patricia frowned as she pulled out a drawer and lifted out two teaspoons. It didn't sound like Gordon was having a conversation with a bank employee—more like he was barking out orders to someone, but who? Surely he didn't talk that way to his personal assistant, Greta. Maybe she should have a word with him about it at a more opportune time. It wasn't fitting for a man in his position to speak to a woman that way. A successful man like Gordon was a soft target for a sexual harassment suit in today's world.

There was a pause as he listened to the person on the other end of the call.

"Don't say a word about it to anyone," Gordon snapped. "I'll be in touch once I get this mess cleaned up."

He ended the call abruptly and slipped the phone back into his pocket.

Patricia grimaced. Was he referring to the mess she had made of things? She eyed him tentatively as she poured their coffees. "Were you able to get the money sent to your account?"

"Yeah, it's all good," Gordon said, drumming his fingers on the granite counter.

"I'm surprised you were able to get a hold of someone at the bank this early," Patricia said, setting a mug down on the counter in front of him.

Gordon threw her an appraising glance. "I'm a private client, Mother. I have the manager's direct line."

"Ah, I see," she said with a nod of acknowledgement as she raised her mug to her lips. Gordon certainly had a considerable amount of clout about town—she'd seen him in action many times. Still, she doubted a bank manager would answer the phone before hours even for a private client. But, what did she know? Given the volatile nature of the situation, it would be best not to press the issue. Gordon was already wound up enough thanks to her misguided collaboration with Tammy. She cleared her throat. "So, are you going to let Ava make the drop once you withdraw the cash?"

Gordon scrutinized the left sleeve of his jacket and carefully brushed it off before flashing her an unsettling grin. "Absolutely. Ava wouldn't dare make off with the money and risk Melanie's life. I only said that for Mallory's benefit. I'm going to play along with this pathetic scam until Melanie is returned to us safely, but I'm going to nail Tammy in the process."

Patricia raised her tapered brows. "What do you mean you're going to *nail* her? You're not going to do anything stupid, are you, Gordon?"

"On the contrary, I plan to be at the Buttercup Campground ahead of the drop so I can expose that thieving piece of garbage for what she is. And then I'm going to sit back and thoroughly enjoy watching old Mallory cuff his own wife and read her her rights—something he should have done a long time ago. If only he knew the half of what that woman's guilty of."

Patricia let out a disapproving gasp. "Do you really think that's wise Gordon, hiding out at the campsite? The police won't be there. The note stipulated that Ava was to come alone. And what if Tammy has an accomplice with her or what if she brings a gun? I know she has one. She told me Mallory insisted she learn how to defend herself when they were first married. If she's capable of kidnapping your child to punish you, she's more than capable of hurting you."

Gordon smirked as he raised his mug of steaming coffee to his lips. "You worry too much, Mother. Tammy's not the only one who can defend herself. I happen to be rather good at it."

Patricia frowned as she sipped her coffee. What did Gordon mean? Was he planning to take a gun to the campground too? She didn't like the sound of this at all. There could be a shoot out, Gordon might be injured or killed, or, if he hurt Tammy, he could end up going to prison—Mallory would make sure of it. The whole situation was getting completely out of hand. She had a sneaking suspicion Tammy wouldn't come to the campsite alone, if she came at all. Five-hundred-thousand dollars was an awful lot of money, more than enough to hire someone to do her dirty work for her.

Not for the first time, Patricia wondered if she should just go down to the station and confess to Mallory what she and Tammy had conspired together to do. Maybe it would be better to face the consequences and let the police handle the situation from here on out. They could arrest Tammy and force her to tell them where she was keeping Melanie. The direction Gordon was moving in was inherently risky. Tammy had outmaneuvered them with the ransom demand, and Gordon was desperate to regain control of the situation, but he was making assumptions that could turn out to be fatal. Patrica had underestimated Tammy once, she didn't intend to make that mistake again. If she couldn't talk Gordon out of his crazy course of action between now and when the drop was scheduled to take place, she would make an anonymous call to 911 and turn Tammy in.

"The bank will be opening any minute now," Patricia said, glancing at the digital clock on the microwave. "Maybe you should head over there."

Gordon drained his coffee and got to his feet. "Thank you, Mother."

"Let me know once you have the money," Patricia said, fussing nervously with her hair. "I won't rest until I know we'll be able to make the drop and get Melanie back."

Gordon leaned over and pecked her on the cheek. "I can promise you one thing, Melanie will be back with us tonight. I intend to make sure of it, one way or another."

14

*M*allory reread the text on Brent's phone, his stomach knotting as his brain whirred into action. Was it only a coincidence that Jeremy had allegedly resurfaced in Brooksbury shortly after disappearing from Alaska? Mallory's experience told him no. Coincidences and criminals didn't belong in the same world together. One way or another, Jeremy Ward was involved in Melanie's disappearance and Mallory intended to find out precisely what role he had played.

"Is something wrong?" Ava asked, her innocent tone at odds with the calculating look in her eye.

Mallory moved his jaw side to side, contemplating whether or not to tell her about Jeremy. He was curious to see her reaction. She had maintained she didn't know him, but Mallory had a strong sense she'd been lying to him for some unknown reason. He couldn't imagine her having an affair with a man like Jeremy Ward, so what exactly was the nature of their relationship? Whatever it was, she was working hard to keep it a secret. "Brent tells me Jeremy

Ward's not living at his last known address in Alaska anymore."

Ava sucked on her lip, as though digesting the news. "So, it's looking more likely that May might have seen her son here after all."

Mallory gave an affirming nod. "It's possible." Given the fact that Jeremy's prints were all over the air compressor, it was more than merely possible, it was highly probable, but Ava didn't need to know that—not until she came clean with him. "I'll have someone track down the vehicle he's driving and put out a BOLO alert just in case." He dialed the station and pressed his phone to his ear. He relayed a few rapid instructions and then hung up.

Ava got to her feet and squeezed her temples as she paced the floor. "You said Jeremy served time for racketeering … I mean if he's behind this then maybe he only wants the ransom money and he won't harm Melanie. At least he's not some pedophile or something." She threw Mallory a cautiously hopeful look, as if waiting on him to alleviate her fears.

He puckered his brow, wondering yet again if Ava Galbraith was really this good of an actress. She played the part of a traumatized mother well but something about her performance still wasn't adding up. The feral fear he'd seen in her eyes the day she'd first reported Melanie missing was gone. The frightened looks she cast him now struck a fraudulent note. But, if she wasn't afraid anymore, that meant she thought Melanie was safe. What was she playing at? Did she know where her daughter was? Was it possible she had made contact with the kidnapper and was keeping it from him? A dangerous decision. He needed her to grasp the gravity of the situation. It wasn't anything she should be attempting to handle on her own, even if she thought she knew the person who had taken her daughter. If he'd learned one thing in this business it was that people were unpredictable.

"Jeremy Ward's a convicted felon and a potentially dangerous suspect," Mallory said. "If things go wrong with the ransom drop, it's anyone's guess what he might do. Melanie's not out of danger yet."

"I understand that. We'll just have to make sure nothing does go wrong," Ava replied with a defiant tilt to her chin. "I'm not going to deviate from the instructions in the note."

Mallory gave a curt nod. "You'll have radio contact with me at all times in case you need backup. The biggest variable we'll be dealing with is the weather. If it starts snowing again, visibility could be next to nothing all the way from the main road down to the Buttercup Campground. And that service road won't be plowed so the snow could be several feet deep, tough to trudge through."

"It won't be a problem for me," Ava assured him. "I'm used to hiking through the snow in the backcountry to take photographs."

The radio crackled on Mallory's hip, Brent's voice breaking through. "I'll be right back," Mallory said, opening the front door and stepping outside the cabin. "What's up?"

"Remember that check you wanted me to run on the Galbraiths' finances?" Brent said.

Mallory peered off at the grayscape horizon. "Yeah, turn up anything?"

"Seems the soon-to-be former Mrs. Galbraith might not be so squeaky clean after all," Brent said. "She took out a loan for two-hundred-and-fifty-thousand-dollars last week."

MALLORY AND BRENT slurped their coffees and studied their notes. They had left Ava at the cabin with a female officer who was walking her through the various stages of the ransom drop, while they waited on Gordon to secure the money and bring it to the station to be marked.

Brent folded his hands behind his head and leaned back in his swivel chair. "What do you make of the loan, boss?"

Mallory rumpled his brow. "It might have no bearing on Melanie's abduction. It could be to hire lawyers to fight for custody. But, it might also mean that Ava's planning on running before the acrimonious divorce battle begins for fear she'll lose custody."

Brent nodded thoughtfully. "Gordon could have threatened her with all the weight of his expensive legal team, or worse. I wouldn't put it past him to threaten his wife with bodily harm. That would be a reason to run—if she's literally scared to death of him."

"So why come back to the cabin to pack up her stuff? I wouldn't do it if I was scared to death of my spouse. There's more to this than meets the eye." Mallory rested one ankle on the edge of his desk and let out a weary sigh. "Melanie was in Ava's care when she disappeared, so Ava could easily have set up the kidnapping with an accomplice. And the ransom note was left on her car, indicating that she's to bring the cash to a remote location. Think about it, Brent. She's gonna need as much money as she can get her hands on if she's planning to leave Gordon and start somewhere afresh with a new identity. She doesn't get all that much with the prenup in place." He scratched an itch on his ear. "Hard to believe a mother would put her own child through something like this for money, but it wouldn't be the first time."

Brent grunted. "How do you think Gordon's going to get half-a-million dollars together in a matter of hours? Must have some fat accounts at the bank to pull that off."

"I've been wondering about that too. He can't withdraw that amount of money all at once, which makes me think he might be drawing on cash reserves he has someplace else.

I've assigned an officer to follow the money trail at the bank if he does show up there, but I'm not counting on it." Mallory tapped his pen on the desk. "Back to Ava Galbraith for a minute. If she's behind the abduction, she didn't act alone. And the timing of Jeremy Ward making an appearance at his parents' place is setting off alarm bells. We need to establish how well Ava Galbraith really knows Jeremy Ward. She claims she's never met him, but I have a hunch they're acquainted." He pulled out his phone from under a pile of papers on the desk and scrolled through his contacts before dialing and hitting the speaker button. "Let's see what Walt Ward has to say about it."

The phone rang five times before Walt picked up. "Hello?"

"Walt, Sheriff Mallory here. I've got a couple of quick questions for you, if you have a minute."

There was muffled whispering on the other end of the line as Walt explained to May who he was talking to. "What can I help you with, sheriff?"

"I'm curious if Ava Galbraith ever met your son, Jeremy?"

A loaded silence presided for a moment or two. "Uh … I'm not sure about that. Gordon went to school with Jeremy of course, but other than that … well, Jeremy's been gone for a long time, as you know."

"Is there any chance Ava could have run into him at some point, at a party, or a neighborhood gathering of some kind?"

Another pause ensued. Mallory raised his brows at Brent.

"Well, let's see," Walt began again, "Jeremy was released December 2015. He spent that Christmas with us before heading off to Alaska. But of course we weren't living here then." He cleared his throat before continuing. "We'd moved out of state, on account of the publicity and all. It was uncomfortable for May going into town with everyone knowing our son was in prison."

"But you kept the cabin here, right? And the land?"

"Yes, we wanted to come back here once I retired and things had settled down again. May and I both grew up here, you see."

"So Jeremy could have visited the property without your knowledge, and he and Ava Galbraith might very well have bumped into one another at some point?"

Walt coughed before responding. "Well ... yes, I suppose that is a possibility."

Mallory gave Brent a knowing nod. "Have you seen Jeremy since his release?"

"No," Walt said. "He doesn't come home anymore, only the occasional call."

Mallory frowned to himself. Walt's voice sounded strained, like he was trying too hard to convince him that Jeremy never visited his elderly parents. It made sense that Walt would want to keep any such visits under wraps. The inhabitants of Brooksbury didn't have fond memories of Jeremy Ward and the trouble he'd brought to town.

"One more thing before I let you go, Walt. Do you use your air compressor much anymore?"

Mallory tapped his fingers on the desk impatiently as Walt hemmed and hawed. "Uh ... no, can't say I do. Were you wanting to borrow it? I think it's buried out there in my workshop somewhere, but I'm sure I could dig it up for you."

"Not necessary, Walt. Thank you, though. I appreciate your time."

Mallory hung up and raised his brows at Brent. "He's lying. He knows very well that May saw Jeremy going into his workshop. I reckon it was Jeremy who used that air compressor. The only question is why?"

Brent scratched his throat. "Flat tire?"

"Or maybe he was blowing up an air mattress for a hostage he was holding in an abandoned cabin somewhere," Mallory said grimly.

Brent let out a low whistle. "Think his old man's covering for him?"

"I don't think Walt really believes Jeremy had anything to do with Melanie's disappearance, but he's probably afraid he'll be a prime suspect once we know he's in town." Mallory glanced at the clock and got to his feet. "Let's take a drive and pay Patricia Galbraith a quick visit while Gordon's working out the money situation. I want to ask her a few more questions without her son hanging over her shoulder monitoring every word she says."

15

*M*allory and Brent pulled into the driveway of Patricia Galbraith's impressive mountain home clad in natural stone and set on a three-acre knoll against a backdrop of snow-daubed granite peaks.

"This pad's got to be worth a pretty penny," Brent muttered to Mallory as he rang the doorbell.

"Word on the street is that Gordon built it for her and paid cash," Mallory replied. "Beats me why he wanted to keep the original family cabin when he could have been living in a palace like this. Nostalgia does funny things to folks."

Patricia answered the door in the same lycra pants and oversized sweater she'd been wearing the previous day. Her ordinarily sleek bob was pulled back in a tortoise shell clip and she clutched a china coffee mug painted with a sprig of pink buds in one hand. Her eyes darted nervously from Mallory to Brent. "What are you doing here? Do you have … I mean, is there any news?"

Mallory gave her a tight smile. "Nothing new to report, I'm afraid. We were just going over the case notes at the station. Can we come in for a few minutes? We have a couple of additional questions you might be able to help us with."

Patricia brushed a manicured hand over her furrowed brow and gestured them inside with a wave of her coffee mug. "Of course, although I'm not sure how I can assist you any further. Gordon's not here. He left a few minutes ago to go to the bank to withdraw the money."

She led them down an arched hallway into an all-white gourmet kitchen with a retro chandelier hanging over a gleaming granite island. Exotic greenery in colorful tubs added splashes of vibrant color to the otherwise snowy perfection of the room. An unopened newspaper lay on the counter. Mallory grimaced when he caught sight of the lead story, *Bring Melanie Home*. The black-and-white picture beneath it was the same one they had used to print up the missing person flyers. He only hoped the story didn't take an even more sinister turn in the next few hours.

Patricia set down her mug and perched uncomfortably on the edge of a bar stool, twisting her hands in front of her. "Have you heard from Justin this morning?"

"No, ma'am," Brent replied. "Rest assured, if he has anything at all to report, he'll contact us right away."

Patricia cast a wary glance from Brent to Mallory. "I suppose there's nothing more we can do in that case until the ransom drop takes place."

Mallory sat down on the bar stool next to her. "Actually Mrs. Galbraith, that's part of the reason we're here. The ransom demand raises a lot of questions. We've had to notify the FBI about it. A kidnapping case is inherently more high-risk than a missing person's case. We could potentially be dealing with a very dangerous person, or persons, when it comes to your granddaughter's abductor."

Patricia's throat bobbed as she waited for Mallory to continue.

"Are you aware of any financial problems your son and daughter-in-law might be having?" Mallory asked, in an overly patient tone. "Or do you know if they owe money to anyone?"

"*Former* daughter-in-law, almost," Patricia corrected him. "And no, they're not hurting for money if that's what you're getting at. Gordon is an excellent provider. Ava and Melanie want for nothing." She blinked rapidly. "He takes excellent care of me as well."

Mallory digested this for a moment, casting a quick glance around the lavish kitchen. Everything Patricia said lined up with what he'd observed about the Galbraiths, but it didn't explain why Ava had recently taken out a loan. If she wasn't hurting for money, then she must want to hide something from Gordon, something that a quarter million dollars could buy.

"When did you find out that Gordon and Ava were planning to divorce?" Brent asked.

Patricia pursed her lips. "Ava's been making life extremely difficult for Gordon for quite some time now, but he kept doing everything in his power to make the marriage work. He told me at Christmas that Ava was bent on filing for divorce although he was still hoping to talk her out of it. He's not a quitter, and the last thing he wanted for that precious little girl of his was a divided home."

Mallory gave a dutiful nod. Having an affair with his PA in the first year of his marriage hardly seemed like the actions of a man who was committed to raising his daughter in an intact home. More like the behavior of a narcissist. Everyone in Brooksbury had caught wind of the affair when Gordon had brought the woman up to the cabin for an illicit weekend and wound up having to call a tow truck after getting his car stuck in the snow. Even Patricia had had a tough time defending his actions that weekend.

"How exactly was Ava making Gordon's life difficult?" Mallory pressed.

Patricia let out a dramatic sigh. "She was forever making ultimatums, threatening to leave if Gordon didn't do what she wanted or give her what she wanted." She wound her fingers together on the counter in front of her. "The worst was when she threatened to take Melanie away from him. That was the knife she twisted most often, and most effectively."

"Do you mean by going after full custody?" Mallory asked.

Patricia angled a brow. "I mean she was prepared to use whatever means necessary to keep Gordon from seeing his daughter."

Mallory and Brent exchanged a quick look.

"Did she threaten him with anything else?" Mallory prodded.

Patricia sniffed and pulled her coffee mug toward her, swilling the contents. "She threatened to ruin his business and sue him for everything he had. No matter how much money Gordon gave her, it was never enough. And she was always accusing him of having affairs with random women he worked with over the years, which was nonsense of course. He learned from his one indiscretion early on in his marriage." Patricia stared defiantly at Mallory over the rim of her mug as she took a sip of coffee.

He jotted down a few notes, feeling more certain by the minute that Patricia was covering something up for Gordon, something she didn't want Mallory to find out about. He didn't know what or why but it felt personal. Surely she couldn't still be holding on to the fact that he had gone on to marry the girl who had dumped Gordon in high school. Why would it bother her? She had never liked Tammy anyway. He rubbed his jaw and plowed on. "Why do you think Ava wants full custody of Melanie?"

Patricia straightened up on her bar stool. "She's a serial liar. She claims that Gordon is emotionally and verbally abusive to her—that he's narcissistic and controlling, and that she and Melanie are in danger. It's a ridiculous charge of course, he's never laid a hand on either of them. He's very protective of them."

Mallory scribbled in his notepad. What Patricia classed as *protective* might be considered by Ava as *controlling*. There had to be a good reason Ava was desperate to get away from him. Gordon had always been a domineering man, and Mallory suspected his ire had been irked when Ava had finally asked him for a divorce. "Have you seen any evidence of this abuse that Ava alleges is happening?"

"Of course not!" Patricia huffed. "Gordon has done everything possible to protect his wife and child, bought them the safest cars, installed the best security systems, you name it. He's never raised a hand against either one of them."

"I see," Mallory said, frowning at his notes. "Do you happen to know if Gordon and Ava had shared bank accounts?"

Patricia drew her brows up to a height of mock outrage. "Gordon's hardly that foolish! They'd be bankrupt by now if he'd agreed to that. Thankfully, he had the sense to protect their assets early on. Ava has a household account and a generous allowance. Believe me, money ran through that girl's fingers like sand!"

Mallory made a mental note of the use of the word *girl*. Both Gordon and his mother were eager to paint Ava as incompetent and negligent, and now greedy. But Ava Galbraith hadn't given him that impression. He suspected there was a sharp intellect and quiet resolve that simmered beneath her timid disposition. Which was part of the reason he couldn't entirely dismiss the idea that Ava had had a hand in Melanie's disappearance.

He leaned forward conspiratorially. "I'm sorry to have to ask you this Mrs. Galbraith, but do you think there is any chance your daughter-in-law could have staged Melanie's abduction?"

A flicker of surprise crossed Patricia's face and she appeared to contemplate the idea with a degree of enjoyment before responding. Her fists clenched on the snowy counter. "I'd go one step further and say it makes perfect sense in retrospect. She wasn't happy with the divorce settlement Gordon proposed, so this could well be how she's going about taking revenge."

Mallory made a few final notes and gave Brent a subtle nod to let him know he was about to wrap up the interview. They weren't going to get an unbiased take on things from Patricia Galbraith. The woman was in complete denial about who her son really was, which also colored her view of her daughter-in-law whom she'd managed to paint in a very unfavorable light. Wherever the truth lay in the tangled web of the Galbraiths' affairs, he couldn't trust Patricia's perspective to be objective.

"Thanks for your help, Mrs. Galbraith," he said, getting to his feet. "We'll keep you posted about the ransom drop as the day progresses. In the meantime, don't go anywhere in case we need to contact you."

Patricia studied him with a calculating look in her eye. "What will you do about the money once Melanie is returned safely. You won't let whoever is behind this get away with it, will you? I mean, it's an awful lot of money for my son to have to front."

"We'll do everything in our power to make sure the perpetrator is brought to justice," Mallory assured her. "And when we do, they'll be charged with kidnapping and extortion. Trust me, they'll be going to prison for a very long time."

Patricia reached for her mug and slid it toward her but she didn't raise it to her lips again. Mallory guessed it was because her hands were shaking too hard to hold it.

16

*B*rent let out a low whistle as he started up the squad car. "That woman made no attempt at all to hide the fact that she hates the very air her daughter-in-law breathes."

Mallory grunted as he clipped in his seatbelt. "Enough to abduct her own granddaughter?"

Brent tilted his head to one side, considering the possibility. "Don't know if I'd go that far, but she's definitely keeping something from us. My hunch is she's protecting Gordon. She might even know who's behind Melanie's disappearance. Could be some unsavory characters Gordon's got himself tangled up with through his business ventures."

"Yeah, she's scared, but defiant at the same time." Mallory said, scrolling through his messages. "Everything Patricia Galbraith does is for the benefit of her son, it's been that way since high school. He was nothing but a punk back then but he never could do any wrong in her eyes. I'm willing to bet she and Gordon are hiding the same secret. You saw the sidelong looks they gave each other when we told them about the ransom note." He let out an exasperated sigh. "If it turns out they're concealing something relevant to Melanie's disappearance, I'll be going after them for obstructing justice."

Brent looked pensive as he pulled out onto the road. "Something else I noticed. Gordon's whole demeanor changed when he found out about the ransom note."

Mallory frowned. "Yeah, I noticed that too. What do you make of it?"

"I'm not sure exactly." Brent drew his brows together in a huddle of concentration. "It was almost as if the ransom note threw him for a loop more than the fact that Melanie was missing. Once he found out about the ransom demand he seemed more angry at the kidnapper, than frightened for his daughter's safety. Odd reaction if you ask me."

Mallory shrugged. "The ransom note made it real, a palpable threat. I get his fatherly rage at the monster who took his daughter."

"Maybe." Brent didn't sound convinced. "I can't put my finger on it but his response struck me as strange. It's as though something dawned on him when he read the note—as though things got personal all of a sudden. I'd venture to say he knows who wrote it."

Mallory threw up his hands in frustration. "Then why doesn't he tell us? Doesn't he want us to find his daughter?"

Brent shook his head. "That's the part I don't get. The only explanation I can come up with is that someone has been blackmailing him for some time now, and the kidnapping is connected to it."

Mallory slipped his phone into his pocket. "That's a thought. And it would explain why he wants to keep us in the dark—although that's a dangerous game to play. Maybe digging into his finances some more will turn up something relevant. Any word on the DNA test on the blood at the cabin yet?"

"Forensics confirmed it's the kid's all right," Brent said. "Not enough to conclude foul play."

"And the nose bleed theory?"

Brent gave a reluctant nod. "Plausible."

Mallory grimaced. "So we can rule out foul play in the cabin at least. Let's head back to the station and do some more investigating while we wait for Gordon to show up with the cash for the drop."

BACK AT THEIR DESKS, Mallory and Brent began combing through the notes they had amassed on the case so far, looking for any new angles they might have missed.

Lost in his work, Mallory glanced up sharply when a junior officer, Hal Morgantini, rapped his knuckles on the open door. "Hey, got a minute, boss?"

Mallory motioned for Hal to join them in the office.

"I've done some snooping around in the Galbraiths' finances like you asked," Hal said. "I'm not done yet but I stumbled onto something that raises a red flag."

Mallory hefted a brow. "Yeah, what you got?"

Hal slapped a file down on the desk. "It's about that two-hundred-and-fifty-thousand dollar loan Ava Galbraith took out. I ran it by the forensic document examiner. His expert opinion is that someone forged Gordon's signature on the paperwork."

Brent let out a shocked whistle. "Bingo! I knew she wasn't being straight up with us."

Mallory picked up the file, frowning as he leafed through it. "What did she take the loan out for?"

"Supposedly to set up a photography business," Hal replied.

Mallory drummed his fingers on his desk. "She's getting a

divorce, she needs to find a way to support herself and her kid. Makes sense to me."

Brent leaned back in his chair and folded his arms in front of him. "Spendy though, wouldn't you say? I reckon you can start a photography business nowadays for the price of a good camera."

"Exactly!" Hal agreed with a note of triumph in his voice. "And get this. She took the loan out against the family cabin which Gordon gets to keep according to the terms of the divorce settlement they're still wrangling over. That's a clear case of fraud right there."

"Good work, Hal. Keep digging," Mallory said. "I want to know everything else there is to know about the Galbraiths' finances. Especially anything to do with Gordon's business ventures. His mother indicated that he and Ava have separate accounts. My hunch is he wanted her kept out of things for very specific reasons."

"What are you getting at, boss?" Brent asked.

"If I had to guess, I'd wager Gordon's business ventures aren't all above board. It would explain why he threatened Ava when she asked for a divorce—he doesn't want his affairs investigated. Even with the prenup in place, she could take him to court if she wanted to and that might make life extremely difficult for him."

Hal furrowed his brow. "It's proving challenging to find out much about Gordon's business empire so far. His network of businesses are a convoluted trail that criss-cross back and forth so many times it's hard to say for sure where exactly the money's coming from."

"Dig harder," Mallory replied. "I'm not sure what's going on here yet, but it's starting to look like there's a bed of criminal activity lurking beneath the Galbraiths' pristine world. If that's the case Melanie might be in the hands of some very dangerous people. And if it turns out either or both of her parents are involved in her abduction in any way, I'm going to nail them for it. Only a truly despicable human being would put their own child through something like this for monetary gain."

"On it." Hal said, disappearing through the door with a genial salute.

Brent ran a hand through his hair. "Child abduction and felony forgery. An infamous pairing. This case is becoming more complicated by the minute."

Mallory nodded thoughtfully. "It's time we had Ava and Gordon Galbraith come in for a polygraph test." He frowned and then added, "Gordon's mother too. This might just turn out to be a family affair. We need to—" He broke off at the sound of Gordon's voice drifting down the hallway.

Mallory locked eyes with Brent. "Here comes the cash. Time to get marking." He got to his feet and lowered his voice. "I want Gordon Galbraith detained at the station until the ransom drop is over. I don't trust him not to interfere with it. Do whatever it takes."

17

The female police officer who had stayed behind at the cabin after Mallory and Brent returned to the station, remained impassive as she adjusted the velcro side straps of Ava's bulletproof vest. In a testament to the officer's training, her voice was unflustered as she ran through everything the ransom drop entailed in a logical and succinct fashion, wholly focused on keeping Ava composed throughout the process. But Ava's stomach wasn't roiling with fear. The fluttering she felt inside was more like anticipation. In fact, she was very much looking forward to this next stage. The card she was about to play next would be entirely unexpected.

True to his word, Gordon had turned up at the sheriff's station mid-afternoon with the full five-hundred-thousand dollars in crisp bills. Ava knew exactly how he'd pulled that off, and it hadn't involved a regulated banking institution as he'd led the police to believe. They weren't stupid though. They had to have their suspicions. They might even have assigned an officer to tail him. But Gordon wasn't stupid either. He would have arranged for a delivery to his hotel room, a nondescript guest checking in or something of that nature. She knew a little of how his world worked from the bits and pieces Jeremy had shared with her about his brief stint in Gordon's employment.

After consulting with the FBI liaison officer assigned to the case, Mallory had been given the go ahead for her to proceed with the ransom drop. Gordon had been detained at the station for questioning when he'd shown up with the money, but Mallory hadn't been forthcoming with Ava as to why. She knew he had his suspicions about the legitimacy of Gordon's business transactions, but she doubted Mallory would show his hand until he had hard evidence, and she would be long gone before that happened. Ava could hardly blame Mallory for not trusting her with his findings. In his eyes, she was still a suspect in Melanie's disappearance. He'd even requested her to submit to a polygraph test earlier that afternoon. No doubt Gordon would be required to do the same. She wasn't worried about it though. He would pass with flying colors just like she had.

"How does that feel?" the female officer asked, grabbing the vest by the shoulder straps and yanking it to make sure it was snug.

"It feels fine," Ava said. "Not too loose, not too tight."

She turned her head as the front door opened in time to see Mallory and Brent stomping the snow from their boots on the mat outside. They tromped into the house and nodded a greeting to the female officer.

"Ready to roll?" Mallory asked.

"She's all set," the officer confirmed, eying the duffle bag in his hand. "I've gone over all the instructions."

"Sure you're still up for this?" Mallory said, as Ava struggled to pull her padded snow jacket over the bulletproof vest.

"Absolutely. Like I told you already, I'll do anything to get my daughter back," she replied, looking him in the eye. The truth was she didn't need Mallory's help, or a bulletproof vest, to make it happen—the plan she had hatched would suffice. Still, the next few hours were critical. Her performance had to be flawless, and that meant playing the part of a terrified mother like never before. She twitched her lips in a wan smile as she passed a shaking hand over her brow.

"You'll do great," Mallory said, with gusto. The other officers nodded in solidarity when he glanced meaningfully at them.

Ava quashed the guilt that rose up inside her at putting them through this charade, and focused instead on the task ahead. Once she had donned her snow boots, hat and gloves, Mallory accompanied her outside, carrying the duffle bag with the money. The temperature was beginning to drop as the day wound down, an iron-gray sky giving way to the charcoal hues of evening. Overhead, an osprey flapped a silent course along the perimeter of the frozen lake, headed for the mountains beyond.

Ava climbed into her station wagon and placed her hands on the wheel. She was already sweating profusely despite the frigid temperature. Mallory opened the passenger door and set the duffle bag on the seat next to her. She glanced in the rearview mirror at the police cruiser parked in the driveway behind her. "You're not going to try and follow me, are you?"

Mallory raised his hands defensively. "We're doing it by the book, just like we agreed. And with the FBI's blessing."

"I know it's important to you to make an arrest," Ava said. "I get that you don't want a kidnapper at large in Brooksbury. But right now the only thing I care about is keeping Melanie alive and I can't let anything jeopardize her safety."

"Don't worry, we're not going to make any moves to pursue the kidnapper until we're sure Melanie is out of danger," Mallory assured her. "Speaking of danger, you know the code word. Remember you're wired, so you can alert us at the first sign of trouble. We have officers on snowmobiles stationed at the next campground two miles south. They can be there in minutes."

"There won't be any trouble. This is going to work," Ava said with a resolute tilt of her chin. "I can feel it in my bones. Melanie's going to be all right."

"Good luck," Mallory said, with a tight smile as he shut the passenger door.

Ava started up the engine and crawled down the lane, her heart beating in wild anticipation. Maybe she shouldn't have projected quite so much confidence that the ransom drop would work. The last thing she wanted to do was alert Mallory's suspicions that the drop was rigged. It was important to stay under the radar until she got the all clear that Melanie was out of harm's way. And there was only one person she trusted to tell her the truth.

As she pulled onto the main road, she inhaled and exhaled slowly to steady her breathing, her gloved fingers gripping the steering wheel tightly. If she pulled this off, she would make everything right again. More importantly, she and Melanie would be home free.

She drove cautiously, her senses wired to a higher frequency than usual. She half-expected a vehicle to come out of nowhere and try to run her off the road, despite the fact that Mallory had made a point of telling her Gordon would be tied up at the station for several more hours. Ava felt certain it was a deliberate ploy on Mallory's part to ensure that Gordon had no opportunity to interfere with the ransom drop after he'd made it abundantly clear that he wasn't comfortable handing the money over to her. She was grateful that Mallory had taken every precaution to make sure she and Melanie were safe throughout. He was a good man, it was a shame he was being deceived by everyone around him, including his own wife.

She smirked as she navigated the route to the campground. Gordon *should* be worried about his money. Even Patricia had chimed in to say that he should be the one to make the drop. Both mother and son had done a good job of painting her as an incompetent wife and negligent mother at every turn. But in the end it would work in her favor if they all underestimated her, especially Mallory.

When she finally spotted the turnoff for the Buttercup Campground, Ava pulled over and parked her car along the main road. She turned off the headlights and sat for a moment staring in the rearview mirror. Satisfied that she was alone, she unzipped the duffel bag, counted out fifty-thousand dollars and stuffed it under the seat before zipping the bag up again with the remainder of the money inside. Her heart was doing double time as she swept the shadows for any sign of unwanted company. Gordon might be tied up at the sheriff's office, but she was certain his henchmen weren't. Someone had delivered that money to him. For several minutes, she sat in the darkness contemplating what she was about to do, and weighing the risks. She would see it through regardless, she wasn't about to back out now, not when what she wanted most was within her reach. This was the only way to make sure she wouldn't have to look over her shoulder for the rest of her life.

Her phone beeped indicating a message. Glancing in the rearview mirror once more, she caught sight of headlights approaching. Her pulse thudded in her temples. She waited until the vehicle pulled up behind her, engine running. Taking a deep breath, she lifted the duffle bag off the seat and checked to make sure her flashlight was in her jacket pocket before climbing out of the car.

Her footsteps crunched in the icy snow as she made her

way back to the dark maroon sedan. Wordlessly, she leaned through the open window and dumped the money into the small carry-on case lying open on the passenger seat. With a quick nod to the driver, she turned and hurried back to her car. Her hands shook as she worked to retrieve the cash she had stashed beneath the seat. As she stuffed it back inside the duffle bag, the sedan pulled away into the skulking twilight.

Despite the icy chill in the air, sweat prickled along the back of Ava's neck as she climbed out of her car again. The entrance gate to the campground up ahead was locked, and the odds of anyone lurking in the vicinity were slim, but she couldn't afford to take any chances. She glanced furtively around, thankful that Mallory had heeded the advice of the FBI liaison officer and brought the time of the ransom drop forward by an hour without informing either Gordon or Patricia. If they had made arrangements for someone to intercept her, it was already too late. One last stop remained before she deposited the duffle bag in the fire ring at campsite 4D.

She switched on her flashlight, skirted around the gate, and began shuffling through the snow along the service road, halting her breathing and listening after every second or third footfall for the sound of anyone following her. When she reached the marker she was looking for, she darted another glance around before stepping onto a hiking trail. She followed it to the first signpost directing her to turn left for Inspiration Viewpoint and right for the Silver Pine Trailhead. Kneeling down, she shone her flashlight around the back of the sign. Buried beneath a mound of snow at the base of the wooden post was a rolled up sleeping bag. She unzipped the duffle bag and hurriedly transferred the fifty-thousand-dollars into a plastic trash bag stuffed deep inside the sleeping bag before rolling it back up again and covering it as best she could.

A grin tugged at her lips as she rummaged around in the snow and gathered up a handful of sticks and pine cones to fill the duffle bag with. She needed the ransom money for other causes, but she could at least supply campsite 4D with enough kindling for the first vacationers of spring to start a fire with.

18

For a long moment, she glared at the unwelcome number displayed on her phone as it vibrated its way across the polished surface of her bedside table. Gritting her teeth, she tapped the keypad and accepted the call. "We had an agreement. You weren't supposed to call this number anymore. You already got your payment from me."

A scoffing laugh was the swift response. "I gave very precise instructions on the ransom note. Unfortunately, it appears they weren't followed."

She shivered despite the warmth of her bedroom. "Not my problem. It was your stupid idea to turn around and demand a ransom in addition to your fee. I know nothing about it. I can't help you there."

"Are you really trying to tell me you didn't know the ransom money was a no show? You expect me to believe that knowing what a conniving, two-faced, lowlife scavenger you are? You ripped me off!"

She wet her lips, a dull gong sounding in her chest. "Are you sure you went to the right campsite?"

A snort of disgust on the other end answered her question. "I

*haven't got patience left for your games, especially not an impro-
vised duffle bag fire starter. That was a particularly low blow. It
makes me feel like you're mocking me, and I don't like people who
mock me. Or people who rip me off. You're the only other person
who knew where and when the drop was taking place."*

*She clutched her phone tighter. The drop had been made. She
was certain of it. She'd got confirmation. What was he playing at?
This was only a ploy to intimidate her. To extract more money. She
got to her feet and paced barefoot across the carpet, rage bubbling
up inside. It wouldn't work. She was the one calling the shots. The
brains behind his brawn. She just needed to remind the moron who
it was he was working for.*

*"So you didn't get what you wanted, suck it up. The ransom
demand was a dumb call, and I wanted no part of it from the
beginning," she hissed. "The cops have a BOLO out on you. The
best thing you can do is carry out the job I paid you to do and then
put your tail between your legs and disappear before you end up
back where you started. You won't make it on the run another
twenty-four hours."*

*"That ten grand won't last me long now that the ransom money
didn't come through. I'm gonna be needing some more cash."*

"Your needs are not my concern."

*The voice hardened, dripping scorn with every syllable. "I know
you're sitting there counting your haul right now. You think you're
so clever pulling one over on me. Maybe I should come over there
and carve that smirk off your pretty little face with my hunting
knife."*

*"You're barking up the wrong tree. I don't have the money. I
didn't intercept the drop."*

*A loaded silence followed. "All right, I'll take a smaller payment
for now, and then you and I will finish this conversation later in
person."*

*"My heart goes out to you in your distress," she continued in a
bored tone. "But I can't help you. I'm tapped out."*

"Yeah, yeah, you told me the whole bleeding hearts story already. I'm not buying it so listen up 'cause I don't like having to repeat myself. Ten grand isn't enough to do the job you want done, not by a long shot, so I'm gonna cut you a deal. Twenty grand and you get the kid back alive."

Her nostrils twitched at the audacity of him. In a matter of weeks, he had morphed into a rapacious monster who was threatening to devour everything she had striven for. He had become more than the minor irritant under her skin that she'd previously dismissed him as. Her breath came in hard, sharp jabs as her mind worked the situation over. She needed to buy some time to flesh out a more robust plan to deal with him once and for all. "You know my circumstances," she said in a conciliatory tone. "It will take a few days to get that amount of money together."

"You're out of time, doll. You'd better figure something out if you want me to keep my mouth shut about your special order."

"Are you threatening me after everything my father did for you? You'd have died in prison if he hadn't taken you under his wing."

"Don't throw that in my face. I did more for your old man than he ever did for me. I'm not threatening you, I'm simply informing you of the new terms of our business arrangement. I need another twenty grand in cash at midnight tomorrow. Bring it in a black duffle bag. I'll be waiting. I'll text you the coordinates when I hang up." He gave a cold chuckle. "That ought to keep me going until I finish typing up my new ransom demand for the Galbraiths."

The line went dead. A moment later, her phone beeped with an incoming message.

38.5195° N, 121.3827° W.

She stared down at the text, drumming the tips of her berry red nails on her bedside table. No one got away with upstaging her. She had a surprise of her own to spring. She would be there tomorrow at midnight if that's what it took to finish this. Then, she would take care of both of her problems at the same time.

To all intents and purposes, Ava had successfully made the trip to the Buttercup Campground and deposited the duffle bag at campsite 4D as the ransom note specified. Now the waiting game had begun.

She fought to keep a smile of elation at bay as Gordon strutted across the cabin floor in front of her flailing his arms angrily while ranting on about how the case had been botched from the outset. He'd been in a particularly foul mood ever since arriving back after spending almost six hours being interrogated, fingerprinted and polygraphed at the sheriff's station.

"No communication yet from the kidnapper," he fumed. "Not a single phone call! What does that tell you? They either have no intention of returning my daughter or they never had her at all. This whole ransom demand is looking more and more like a scam—just some bottom feeder who knows I have means and is taking advantage of the situation." He thumped his fist on the kitchen counter for emphasis, rattling the fruit platter centerpiece in the process. "Now, they have my money and my daughter's still missing, thanks to the incompetence of the entire sheriff's department, not to mention the idiocy of the FBI in sanctioning the drop before they got here!"

Ava raised her brows in an apologetic gesture when Mallory shot a quick look her way.

"You may be right that the ransom request was a con job, someone who was manipulating the situation for his or her own ends," Mallory said, his face a picture of professional calm. "There are a lot of things that don't add up." He cleared his throat before adding, "You should be aware that we're bringing your mother down to the station to take a polygraph test too." He glanced at his watch. "In fact, she's probably there right now."

A bolt of anger coursed over Gordon's pinched face. "How dare you go behind my back and orchestrate a sham interrogation like that!" He wagged a finger menacingly in Mallory's face. "You've always had it in for my mother ever since she sent Tammy packing. Let me tell you something, I'll have my lawyers crawling all over you for this come morning. It's slanderous to even insinuate my mother had anything to do with kidnapping her own granddaughter!"

Mallory squared his jaw. "Retaining a lawyer would be advisable."

"Believe me, I fully intend to hire a legal team that will put an end to your lackluster career once and for all." Gordon stomped over to the front door and wrenched it open. "I'll have your badge for this, Anderson, mark my words. You've held a grudge against me ever since I dated Tammy in high school. Well let me tell you something, she wasn't worth the price of a cheap dinner."

A deep flush crept up Mallory's neck. "After all these years, you still can't accept the fact that she dumped you, can you, Galbraith?"

Gordon threw back his head and guffawed. "Is that what

she told you? That she actually *chose* you instead of me? I guess she knew your sad little ego couldn't handle the truth. Hate to shatter your illusions, but I was the one who sent her packing, and you just happened to be the doormat lying around for her to wipe her feet on."

Without waiting for Mallory to respond, Gordon slammed the front door behind him and, a moment later, Ava heard the sound of his engine revving as he tore out of her driveway and up the lane toward the main road. He was most likely already calling his lawyers, and making a beeline for the station before Patricia said something she wasn't supposed to.

"I'm so sorry," Ava said, choking the words out. "He was completely out of line insulting your wife like that."

"Forget it," Mallory said, a hard set to his jaw. "Gordon hasn't changed one iota from our high school days. He's still as arrogant now as he was back then. Don't worry, he can throw his weight around all he wants, but his threats won't deter me from getting to the bottom of what's going on. He knows something about Melanie's abduction that he's not telling me, and so does his mother."

Ava rumpled her brow. "Do you really think Patricia could do something so egregious as keeping information from us that might help us find Melanie? I mean, she is her grandmother after all. She may hate me with a passion, but I can't deny she loves Melanie to pieces."

Mallory grunted. "She's equally obsessed with her son—obsessed enough to do almost anything for him. And she made it pretty clear to me that she thought you were out to take Melanie away from Gordon. She could have hired someone to abduct her granddaughter. Patricia Galbraith certainly has motive. The puzzling part is the ransom. It's not your typical custody battle tactic."

"Maybe it was to throw you off her trail?" Ava suggested,

pulling a befuddled face. "She could have sent her accomplice to pick the money up again afterward."

Mallory shook his head. "I don't think she had anything to do with the ransom. She seems pretty eager for us to go after the kidnapper and retrieve Gordon's money as soon as Melanie is released."

Ava pulled at a strand of her hair and let out a beleaguered sigh. "If she knows where Melanie is, at least she won't let anyone hurt her."

Mallory grimaced. "Not intentionally. But, she might make some more foolish decisions and put Melanie's life in danger. That's why we're bringing her in to do the polygraph. I want to find out once and for all what she knows about her granddaughter's disappearance."

Ava fixed a sober gaze on Mallory. "Do you think there's a possibility Gordon was in on it with her?"

Mallory rubbed a hand over his face. "Hard to believe a father would deliberately put his kid through something so traumatic, but I wouldn't put anything past Gordon. The ransom may have been part of a bigger scheme. We're investigating his finances and there are several red flags."

Ava made a point of widening her eyes, even though she knew exactly what Mallory was alluding to. "What do you mean? What kind of red flags?"

"His business ventures are suspect, for the most part. The irregular money trail we've uncovered so far speaks to money laundering, trafficking, and racketeering. It could go all the way back to what Jeremy Ward was caught up in and convicted of years ago. We never did find out who was running the whole operation. For some reason, Jeremy chose not to squeal." Mallory hesitated as if wrestling with a decision. "I know your name's not on any of the businesses or accounts, but if there's something you want to tell me, now would be a good time to come clean."

Ava averted her eyes from Mallory's accusatory stare. "I'm ... completely in the dark. I don't know anything about Gordon's business dealings. He keeps all that from me. We have a joint household account, and I have an allowance, but that's about it. And I don't stand to gain anything from the divorce, thanks to the prenup."

Mallory let out a humph. "The way things are going, it's a blessing your name's not on anything. I'd advise you to contact your lawyer anyway. You could be implicated in whatever we uncover if you don't retain legal counsel. I'm waiting on a search warrant for Gordon's properties, residential and commercial. Once it comes through, we'll comb through everything, soup to nuts, including this place."

"The cabin?" Ava's skin tingled all over. "But, you already searched it."

Mallory threw her a sharp look. "For a missing child. You can hide drugs, money—even weapons—in a lot smaller spaces than a child can crawl into. You'd be surprised how creative people become when they want to hide illegal goods."

No, actually, I wouldn't. Ava swallowed the knotted ball in her throat. "So when you say search, are you going to tear the place apart, like they do on TV?"

Mallory raised his brows. "Do you have any objections if it helps us get to the bottom of who took your daughter?"

"Uh, no, of course not." Ava fought to keep from babbling. "I'm just in shock, that's all. I mean, I had no idea Gordon's business was anything less than reputable. He was already very successful when I married him. I thought ... well, he seemed to be well-respected by everyone."

The words were barely out of her mouth before the door to the cabin opened again and Brent and two other officers walked in. Brent held aloft some paperwork before slapping it down on the counter. "Got the warrant, boss.

We've dispatched officers to the premises in Cedarville also."

Mallory turned to Ava, a questioning look on his face. "With your permission?"

She waved a dismissive hand at him before sinking down on the couch and clutching a cushion to her churning stomach. "Yes, absolutely. Do whatever you have to do."

Everything would be all right, she reassured herself as she watched the officers move off through the cabin. If they found it, she would just have to make her next move quickly. Before they figured out it wasn't connected to Gordon.

20

*W*ith the help of the additional officers, Mallory managed to wrap up the search of the cabin in a little under two hours. The mess they had made, on the other hand, would take days to clean up. Once they'd discovered the stash of cash, they had been forced to tear into everything. Ava had remained unnaturally calm when the young crew-cut officer walked into the cabin with his arms piled high with French loaves from the freezer in the garage. "All stuffed with bills, sir," he announced with thinly disguised enthusiasm.

"Bills?" Mallory echoed, scarcely believing what he was hearing. What had started out as a missing person's case was shaping up to be more like something straight out of a mob movie, and nothing at all like the kind of low level crime he was used to dealing with in Brooksbury.

"All hundred dollar bills, from what we can tell," the officer continued. "No idea yet how much we're looking at."

Mallory grimaced. "All right, notify the FBI. I want all Gordon Galbraith's accounts frozen immediately. And bring him back in for questioning."

Mallory shot a look at Ava who had been busy zipping the covers back on the cushions on her couch. Her expression was a seamless blend of innocence and shock that perfectly matched the narrative she was holding to. She sank down on the couch, passing a shaking hand over her brow. "I just can't believe it. Is it … is it the ransom money?"

Mallory examined some of the bills. "They're not marked. This cash wasn't part of the ransom drop. It could be tied to one of Gordon's shady business ventures—money laundering most likely." He grimaced. "Which means he's involved himself with some unsavory characters, drug dealers would be my guess."

Ava shook her head slowly. "I never suspected for a moment that he was doing anything illegal."

Mallory silently handed the bills back to the officer. He hadn't told Ava yet that he'd uncovered her own shady loan deal. For now, he would let her think he assumed the money they'd found was Gordon's. But if the bills in the freezer turned out to match the amount of the loan Ava had taken out, he would have probable cause to bring her in for questioning on suspicion of forgery and fraud. He still wasn't sure if the loan was connected to Melanie's abduction, but he would use the opportunity to grill Ava on what was really going on at the cabin by the lake, and hopefully, in the process, piece together what had happened to little Melanie.

Moments later, a ginger-haired officer appeared in the kitchen, eyes bulging. "Sir, you might want to come and take a look at this."

"Wait here," Mallory said to Ava. He followed the officer out to the garage where part of the roofing was dangling down. On the chalky floor below, amid chunks of drywall, sat an assortment of black plastic cases of varying sizes.

"Money and weapons, sir," the ginger-haired officer said

with a feverish excitement in his voice. "A much more impressive stash than the cash we found in the freezer."

Mallory swiped a hand over his jaw. "I want this kept under wraps from Ava Galbraith for now."

The officer threw him a questioning look. "You don't think she knows about it?"

"I have no idea what she knows for sure," Mallory said. "But I'd like a chance to question her before I share the full extent of what we've dug up around here. Back your cruiser up to the garage and get this stuff out of here on the QT."

"YOU LOOK EXHAUSTED," Mallory said to Ava, after Brent and the other officers had finished wrapping things up in the garage and taken off. "You should probably get some sleep."

Ava chewed on her lip. "I'm still in shock about the money in the freezer. I can't get my head around the idea that Gordon is involved in money laundering." She frowned, as if a thought had just struck her. "Do you think he owes money to these people he's got himself tangled up with?" She let out a heart-wrenching moan. "If some drug dealer has taken Melanie, she could be in real danger. Who knows what they're capable of doing, even to a child?"

Mallory grimaced inwardly. Whatever Ava was imagining, it was worse. Much worse. The conversation he'd had with the FBI liaison officer had been a sober reminder. If it turned out Gordon Galbraith owed these people money, he might not be getting his daughter back in one piece.

"We'll take Gordon back in for questioning, but we won't arrest him yet," Mallory explained. "It would only alert whoever he's working with to the fact that we're on to them, and that might put Melanie in even more danger."

Ava clapped a hand to her mouth.

"We'll find these people, no matter what it takes," Mallory assured her. "The FBI is sending a team to assist us. They'll be here tomorrow, weather permitting."

His phone buzzed and he glanced at the screen. He needed to take this call but not in earshot of Ava. "I'll be back early in the morning. Do you want me to arrange for a female officer to stay with you tonight?"

Ava shook her head. "No, I'll be fine. I won't be able to sleep knowing there's someone milling around in my house."

Mallory bade her goodnight and headed out to his car, pressing his phone to his ear. "Go ahead, Brent."

"I've got the polygraph results on the Galbraiths." He hesitated before adding in a somber tone. "Patricia Galbraith is lying about Melanie's abduction."

MALLORY PULLED into his garage still mulling over the day's developments. It didn't come as any great surprise to him to learn that Patricia Galbraith was fabricating parts of her story. What he needed to figure out was why. He sighed as he leaned his head wearily on the steering wheel. He would start on the case again first thing in the morning. For now, he had personal problems of his own to worry about. Brent's sister, the assistant manager at his local bank and a good friend, had left him a voice mail earlier and he was still reeling from its contents.

"I know it's none of my business, Mallory, but I thought you ought to know that your savings account's been over-drawn by almost four-thousand-dollars for the past several days. You're being hit by fees left, right, and center for automatic payments and bounced checks coming in. Looks like someone made a withdrawal for ten-thousand-dollars and you didn't have enough in the account to cover it. Let me know if you want me to transfer any funds for you and I can see about waiving some of those fees."

Mallory had racked his brains trying to think through the possibilities on the drive home. Tammy must have made the withdrawal. Why hadn't she told him about it? More importantly, what could she possibly need such a large sum of money for? Maybe he'd been right to question all that time she was spending on her phone of late. The gaming could be a cover for something a lot more insidious, like online gambling, or a shopping addiction—she could be hiding all the parcels that were arriving during the day and he'd be none the wiser.

The house was dark and quiet when he opened the door that led from the garage into the kitchen and tiptoed inside. He padded down the hallway to the guest bedroom and peered around the door, listening to the intermittent high-pitched sound that escaped through Tammy's parted lips. He watched the rise and fall of the duvet for several minutes to make sure she was in a deep sleep. He felt bad about what he was about to do, but he needed to know what she was up to. If it turned out she had a gambling addiction, he would do everything he could to help her if she was willing to seek treatment. But, if she was planning on cleaning him out before she filed for divorce she could think again. He had worked too hard to build the life they enjoyed together in Brooksbury to watch it fritter away to nothing. Tammy may not think he had accomplished much in his career, but he was content with his role as a small town sheriff. He enjoyed the gentle pace of life in Brooksbury and the meaningful relationships he had built up over the years with the good-hearted folk he served.

After taking a shallow breath, Mallory padded over to the chest of drawers at the bottom of the bed and quietly disconnected Tammy's phone from the charger. Her gentle whistling snore continued unabated and he slipped out of the room undetected. Safely back in the kitchen, he sat down at the dining table and punched in her four-digit passcode. She hadn't volunteered it to him, but he'd discreetly watched her tap it in with a berry-colored fingertip as they sat on the couch one evening watching a movie together. He'd been trying to catch a glimpse of what she was doing, irked that she couldn't seem to leave her wretched phone alone for even a few minutes, but she'd quickly slipped it into her lap once she realized his eyes weren't glued to the TV screen.

He went straight to Tammy's browser history and began leafing through her open tabs, searching for any indication that she was gambling online or that she'd become a closet shopaholic, but he could find nothing untoward; recipe searches, directions to a doctor's office, YouTube exercise videos. It looked like she hadn't accessed their bank accounts from her phone recently. Could their account have been hacked? He opened her photos next, trawling through dozens of innocuous pictures, a few selfies, and some pictures she'd taken of random items, including a bottle of nail polish.

He exited her photos and tapped on the phone icon next. Scrolling through her most recent calls, he frowned when he noticed multiple calls to and from Patricia Galbraith. What on earth was Tammy talking to Gordon's mother about? They didn't even converse in public on the rare occasions when they ran into each other. Tammy couldn't stand the woman after the way she'd been treated by her when she and Gordon were dating back in high school. A niggling doubt wormed its way into his thoughts as Gordon's scathing laugh echoed in his mind.

Is that what she told you?

Could he really trust what Tammy said about either of the Galbraiths? Was she the one who had broken it off with Gordon all those years ago, or was it the other way around? Mallory tugged his fingers through his hair in frustration. It shouldn't matter anymore. It was old history. The more pressing question was why Patricia Galbraith was contacting his wife? After everything he'd uncovered so far, he didn't trust Gordon's mother. He grimaced at the irony of it. He didn't trust his own wife either—why else was he checking her phone? He hurriedly scanned the rest of Tammy's recent calls, frowning at an unknown out-of-town number she'd called several times in the last couple of days. He made a note of the number to run a check on it at the station, and then opened her text messages. His eye was immediately drawn to another number that wasn't in her contacts.

What did u expect? quit texting me!

Tammy: *I won't accept this is the end. You need me.*

And you need help!

Tammy: *Are you worried about Mallory?*

Are you kidding me? That loser still thinks you picked him over me!

Mallory stared at the screen in disbelief. Stomach churning, he reread the last line again more slowly to make sure he wasn't misunderstanding it. Gordon had hurled that very same insult at him earlier today. But, it couldn't be true, could it? Tammy and Gordon together, after all these years. He rubbed his thumb into his throbbing temple, trying to clear his thinking. It would explain why Tammy and Patricia were in contact with one another. Patricia must know about the affair. That was what she was hiding from him. But, it didn't explain the money Tammy had withdrawn. Were the two things even connected? Mallory shut off the phone and set it down on the counter, his thoughts spinning out of control. Rage boiled up from deep within, dulling the pain of betrayal.

All this time he'd been doing everything in his power to save his marriage while Tammy had been making a mockery of it, hooking up with the man she'd sworn she left for him seventeen years ago.

*L*ess than an hour after the officers had wrapped up their search of the cabin and departed for the night, Ava's phone began to vibrate. She glanced down at the number on the screen and sucked in a breath. A ripple of apprehension snaked across her shoulders. She was on the verge of finding out if they had succeeded—or if everything had gone awry. She desperately needed this to be good news. There was no backup plan, no escape hatch through which she could extricate herself from the mounting danger she was in. Steeling herself for whatever report she was about to get, she picked up her phone and swiped her finger across the screen. "Did you get the money?" Her voice came out in a breathless whisper even though she was alone in the cabin.

"Yeah, we're all good. You'll find what you asked for in the wooden toolbox on the top shelf of my old man's workshop. I think you'll be more than satisfied with our trade."

"And the delivery?"

"The package arrived safely at its destination."

Ava closed her eyes and blew out a silent breath of relief, the knot in her stomach unraveling as it sank in. She had dared to hope her plan would work, yet doubt had dogged her every step of the way.

The phone shook in her hands but her voice held steady. "Then it's time to turn up the heat. You know what we discussed."

"The rendezvous has already been set up."

She carefully tucked a strand of hair behind her ear. "And Gordon?"

"He'll get the coordinates from a burner phone."

"Good." Ava let out another shallow breath. "The police tore the cabin apart. They found the money in the freezer in the garage. I can't give you a cut of that anymore."

There was a long pause on the other end of the line. "The cops won't connect it to you. They'll think it's part of Gordon's money laundering operation. It can only work in your favor. Besides, we don't need it now anyway. The ransom demand was a genius addition to the plot. We both got enough out of it to take care of things."

Ava combed her fingers through her hair. It was certainly more than enough for what she had in mind. "I think the police are closing in on Gordon."

"It'll be his lucky day if they get to him before I do."

Ava grimaced. "So, what are you going to do now?"

"Disappear. For good this time. South, where it's warmer. And you?"

"Same. Some place warmer. I want to feel the sand between my toes. I don't care if I never see snow again."

For a moment or two there was silence between them, and then the voice on the other end of the line said, "I take it I can get rid of this phone after tonight?"

"Yes," Ava said, "I won't be calling you again. Thank you for everything, and good luck wherever you end up."

"Well you know what they say, *the enemy of my enemy is my friend.* It was a pleasure doing business with you."

Ava ended the call and studied her badly-bitten finger-nails. It was almost over. It had required an intricate dance of fact and fiction. Strategy and risk. But, in the end, she would walk away with what she wanted, and everyone else would get what they deserved. The final curtain had yet to fall, but Gordon's demise was inevitable. He had chosen the wrong dance partner.

She walked over to the coat rack and quickly donned her outerwear. It was time to pay a nocturnal visit to Walt Ward's workshop and pick up the last piece of evidence she needed to bring her husband down.

22

*M*allory spent a sleepless night on the couch with Tammy's phone stashed under one of the cushions. After the shocking discovery of her infidelity, he hadn't been able to bring himself to climb the stairs to the master bedroom and sleep in the bed they had once shared as man and wife. More importantly, if he slept on the couch, there was no chance of Tammy slipping out of the house unbeknownst to him. It was time to have it out with her, no matter where that conversation took them. He was sick of the minefield of lies that separated them.

At five-thirty the next morning, he fished Tammy's phone out of the couch, pocketed it, and pulled himself to his feet. Head pounding, he made his way into the kitchen and brewed a pot of strong coffee. He hadn't worked out yet how best to broach the topic of the sizable cash withdrawal from their account, not to mention Tammy's betrayal with Gordon. He felt like a fool when he thought back to how sincerely he had sympathized with Ava Galbraith over the breakdown of her marriage, never imagining his own wife was the one who was carrying on with Gordon. Mallory grimaced. He didn't know for sure if Ava knew it was Tammy, but she must have had her suspicions. Maybe that's what she'd been keeping from him all along. He had sensed a level of evasiveness in her interactions with him, an unwillingness to look him in the eye at times. He could only imagine how difficult it must have been for her to be forced to work together with him under such awkward circumstances, knowing what she did about Gordon and Tammy.

When the coffee finished percolating, he poured himself a steaming mug and sat down wearily at the dining table. Another fear had wormed its way into his ragged thoughts during the long, restless hours of the night. He slurped a mouthful of coffee as he pondered it. The notion that Tammy might know something about Melanie's disappearance was disturbing to say the least. But feasible. If she was involved with Gordon, and in communication with Patricia, she might have picked up on what they were up to. Worse, what if she was involved somehow? He rammed a hand through his hair. He had no idea what his wife was capable of anymore. Could she have used the money she had withdrawn to pay someone to abduct Melanie? The thought filled him with dread. She knew how he felt about the kind of people who were willing to exploit children. If it turned out that she had something to do with Melanie's disappearance, he wasn't sure he would be able to stop himself from hurting her.

Startled out of his reverie by a footfall in the hallway, he reached for his coffee mug and steeled himself for the impending showdown.

"You're up early," Tammy exclaimed, her voice more high-pitched than the hour or the observation warranted. Her eyes darted around the room with a frenetic tick.

"Looking for this?" Mallory asked, pulling her phone out of his pocket and setting it on the table in front of him. He took another sip of coffee as he watched her reaction; the angry twitch of a muscle in her cheek, the rapid narrowing of her eyes, the defiant swish of her sleek, black hair over one shoulder, the rigid posture—more noticeably, the complete lack of shame. He clenched his jaw, willing himself to remain calm.

"You took my phone?" she said in a low threatening tone that Mallory gauged to be close to boiling. He had become adept at recognizing the temperature of conversations between them.

"I know everything, Tammy," he said evenly. "There's no point in denying it."

Her eyes widened momentarily, and then glinted with anger. "What exactly did your snooping reveal that you didn't already know?"

"Well it certainly cleared up why you never want to talk about us anymore. And why you replaced Ava Galbraith's framed photos that I bought at the fair with those hideous prints. You're still obsessed with Gordon, aren't you? You married me and then hooked up with him again behind my back."

Ignoring the accusation, she held out her hand for her phone. "You had no right to invade my privacy!"

"I have every right to know what's going on when it involves my hard-earned money," Mallory retorted. "Just what exactly were you planning to do with that cash you withdrew from our account? An exotic getaway with Gordon? Or are you emptying out our accounts before you dump me, is that your grand scheme?"

Tammy stomped angrily across the floor and reached out her slim, tapered fingers to snatch up her phone from the table, but Mallory scooped it up first and gripped it tightly in his fist. "You'll get this back when we've finished our conversation, which we're going to have whether you like it or not, so you might as well take a seat and answer a few questions." He gestured to the chair next to him but Tammy folded her arms across her chest and glared at him.

He held her gaze. "How long has it been going on?"

She smirked. "I hate to break it to you but you're really not cut out to be a detective, Mallory. How could you not have known that it never ended? Gordon and I are two halves of a perfect whole. I understand him in ways his insipid wife couldn't even begin to comprehend."

Mallory recoiled inside at the words that flew from her lips like spinning blades, but he kept his composure, determined to get some answers to his most burning questions. "If you loved him so much why did you break it off with him in high school?"

Tammy arched a defiant brow. "I didn't. He wanted to marry me but his overbearing mother interfered with our plans and convinced him that his future children would end up as felons if he walked down the aisle with me."

Mallory quietly digested her words. So Gordon had told the truth about that after all. A knot twisted in his stomach. Tammy had married him out of convenience. He was the clean-up crew who'd been willing and available to sweep her out of the trailer park she'd grown up in and into a zip code of respectability, but nothing more. He didn't really know the woman he had married at all. He had loved a stranger all these years. The growing realization left him feeling like he was drowning in her deception, suffocating beneath a tapestry of lies skillfully woven into a cheap fabric that had become their life together. He winced as he swallowed the hard lump in his throat. "Did you ever love me, Tammy? Try telling the truth for once."

A whisper of irritation on her botoxed brow answered the question for him. "If you must know, you were only ever the backup plan," she said tartly. "It was Gordon I wanted all along."

"And now he doesn't want you," Mallory said, his voice falling away.

Tammy gave a testy laugh. "That won't last, it never does. Gordon Galbraith can't stay away from me. It's the part of the game he loves the most. I'm his soul's reflection. We're two forces who are bound together for time and eternity."

Mallory stared at her agape. "A *game*? You think this is all a game? You married me, Tammy, for better or for worse. We took vows to commit ourselves to one another. I loved you with everything I had and you used that against me."

She uncrossed her arms and walked over to the coffee pot. "Get over yourself, Mallory. You're acting like you're back in high school pouting over a football play that didn't go your way. It's tiresome."

Mallory studied his wife as she poured herself a coffee. Tall, willowy, beautiful Tammy. Of course he had noticed her in high school. Along with every other guy on the football team. He'd been ecstatic when she'd agreed to go out on a date with him, elated when she chose him over Gordon Galbraith, and moved to tears the day she'd promised herself to him under a flower-bedecked arbor overlooking the lake in the grounds of the Sandyfield Inn. He fought to steady the tremor in his voice as he asked, "Are there others, besides Gordon? That unknown number you've been calling, who is that?"

She stiffened and her fingers clenched the handle of her mug tightly before she answered with a forced air of nonchalance. "Like I said before, you had no right to take my phone and it's none of your business who I talk to."

"It is when you associate with people I'm investigating—Patricia Galbraith for instance. What's that all about? I thought you hated her. Are you trying to get her to put in a good word with Gordon for you, or is there something else going on that I should know about?"

Tammy set her mug down on the counter, a calculated look in her eyes. "As a matter of fact, she's been hounding me lately. The woman's deranged—obsessed with her son and granddaughter. She knew Gordon and I were having an affair and that Gordon and Ava were getting divorced. She wanted to make sure Gordon got custody of Melanie. She's been asking me a lot of questions recently about how the police investigate missing children cases." Tammy frowned as she walked back over to the table and sat down on the chair next to Mallory, leisurely crossing her long legs. "I though it was very odd."

Mallory waited for her to continue. He had an uneasy feeling he knew what she was going to say next.

Tammy stared into her coffee mug as if collecting her thoughts. "That's why when Melanie went missing, and Gordon was beside himself with worry, I had to make sure Patricia hadn't gone and done something stupid. I called her up and asked her outright if she'd taken Melanie, but she denied it." Tammy tilted her head to one side. "The thing is, I'm almost certain she's lying."

Mallory sat up a little straighter, one hand instinctively checking for his walkie talkie. "What do you mean? Why do you think she's lying?"

"I went over to her place to confront her. Of course she swore she knew nothing about Melanie's disappearance, but —" Tammy's voice trailed off and she gave Mallory a look that made him shiver inside.

"Don't toy with me when there's a missing kid at stake," he growled.

Tammy let her shoulders sag as though relenting with reluctance, a gesture Mallory had seen a thousand times before and knew could be deceptive. Her voice dropped to a confiding whisper. "I saw a purple hat with a pom pom hanging on the coat rack inside her front door. I could have sworn it was the same one Melanie was wearing in the missing poster." She traced her fingers delicately around the rim of her mug. "Unless of course, Patricia knit her more than one."

Mallory swore and got to his feet, yanking his walkie talkie from his belt. "Why didn't you tell me about this before?"

Tammy stalled before answering, leaning back on the legs of her chair and eyeing him coolly. "I wasn't sure if Gordon was in on it—if it was some kind of attempt to discredit Ava so he could get custody of Melanie. I didn't want anything to happen to him."

Mallory grimaced. "You'd put that cheating scumbag ahead of a four-year-old child's safety? Who are you anyway? You're certainly not the woman I thought I married. Not by a long shot." Every part of him longed to reach for his wife and shake her by the shoulders until her teeth rattled around in her head. But, he wasn't that kind of man, and he wasn't about to sink to her level.

For now, he needed to put his own problems aside. In light of what Tammy had told him, it was imperative that he bring Patricia Galbraith in for questioning again. "We're not done yet," he called back to Tammy as he strode out of the kitchen. "You still haven't told me what you did with that ten grand."

23

The hard, plastic chair she was sitting in rocked unsteadily every time Patricia shifted position. A paper cup of lukewarm coffee sat untouched on the utilitarian table in front of her. She had requested coffee with cream, not this sand-colored fluid with powdered clumps bobbing around on the surface like flotsam. Opposite her sat a stone-faced Sheriff Mallory. He had asked her to come down to the station early this morning to provide assistance with some details about the case, but Patricia had a sneaking suspicion there was more to it than that. He knew something. Gordon certainly wouldn't have told him what she had done, so that left only Tammy. Patricia pressed her lips together, inwardly berating herself for the umpteenth time for ever collaborating with that no good piece of trailer trash. Had Tammy confessed everything to Mallory, or given him some limited version of the truth? If he knew about the plot to kidnap Melanie, then Patricia was resolved to incriminate Tammy as the instigator. But it was also possible that Mallory had unearthed something unbeknownst to his wife. Patricia would have to tread cautiously. Gordon had warned her not to speak to Mallory again without enlisting one of the lawyers he had on retainer, but Patricia had been afraid it would only make her look guilty to show up with a lawyer in tow. She needed to find out what line of inquiry Mallory was pursuing first.

"Thanks for coming down to the station, Mrs. Galbraith," Mallory began. "I'd like to take a few minutes and go over the timeline of Melanie's disappearance with you once more, if you don't mind."

Patricia relaxed a little and shrugged. "If you must, I suppose, but I'm not sure I can add anything to what you already know."

Mallory gave her an ingratiating smile. "Let's start at the beginning. When exactly did you come back from your trip to Chicago?"

Patricia frowned in concentration, even though she knew precisely when she'd arrived back, down to the exact hour—she had planned it very carefully after all. "Let's see, I believe it was Wednesday night around eleven or so. I changed my ticket at the last minute because I wanted to be back before that storm hit in case my flight got cancelled."

"And originally you were due back when?"

"Not until Sunday evening." She gave a rueful grin. "The weather in Chicago was so dreadful it really wasn't much of a hardship to cut my trip short. I don't like shopping when it's cold and miserable."

"I see." Mallory studied his notes for a moment or two before looking up again. "And what time on Thursday did you learn that Melanie was missing?"

Patricia pulled out a tissue and dabbed at her eyes, heaving her chest up and down like it had just hit her all over again that her granddaughter was missing. "Gordon texted me. It was six minutes after one in the afternoon. I'll never forget that, it was the worst moment of my life. He'd left me several messages before that, but I'd put my phone on the charger in the bedroom and forgotten all about it. I was busy unpacking and doing laundry." She suppressed a sob. "I remember just staring at the clock on the mantel in disbelief, wondering how life could possibly go on when Melanie was missing." She sniffed and looked up at Mallory. "It's the worst pain in the world when anything happens to one of your own."

Mallory gave a wooden-faced nod. "And you didn't see Melanie at any point on Thursday?"

Patricia furrowed her brow, blinking in exaggerated surprise at the question. "No. How could I have? She'd been missing since early that morning when that negligent mother of hers—"

Mallory pinned a disapproving gaze on her as he cut her off. "Can you describe what Melanie was wearing that day?"

Patricia painted on a puzzled expression, her heart fluttering a little faster in her chest. "Oh, you mean the clothes in the missing poster?"

Mallory nodded encouragingly. "Yes, any additional description you can give us would be useful. It's hard to pick up everything from a photo but most women tend to have a good eye for detail."

Patricia tilted her head to one side as she gave it some thought. "Well, she had on her purple and teal jacket that Gordon bought her last Christmas from that expensive ski shop in Cedarville. Hmmm, let's see … her matching snow pants and purple leggings, her furry snow boots that she insisted on wearing everywhere, and of course her purple pom pom hat that I knit for her." Patricia gave a weak smile. "She loves everything purple. Last year it was pink. Everything has to match or she refuses to wear it. She's always been my little fashionista—loves to shop, that one."

Mallory furrowed his brow and tapped his pen on the table as if deep in thought.

Patricia reached for the paper coffee cup and put it to her lips but couldn't commit to taking a sip, recoiling at the thought of the clotted fake cream dissolving on her tongue. Even the smell of the cheap, lukewarm coffee nauseated her. This was not an environment she belonged in. The very fact that she was here in this nasty room at all was testament to the folly of associating with anyone who'd grown up in a trailer park. She silently admonished herself for failing to heed her own advice. Apparently, Gordon hadn't taken it either. Somehow, Tammy had managed to get her claws into both of them.

"Mrs. Galbraith," Mallory said, setting down his pen after a thoughtful pause and clasping his hands together in front of him. "How did you know Melanie was wearing purple leggings when she went missing?"

Patricia opened her mouth and then closed it again. Heat rose in her cheeks as she frantically ran back through what she'd told Mallory. Yes, she had mentioned the leggings. She'd been trying too hard to appear helpful, and had over-played her hand. She willed herself to remain calm. A stupid mistake, but not a critical one. She would simply play the flustered Grandma. "Well … I mean I just assumed. She always wears her purple leggings under her snow pants. You wouldn't believe the fuss she raises when her clothes don't match."

Mallory gave a polite chuckle, then rubbed a hand over his jaw as if deliberating on something. "Changing gears for a moment, did my wife happen to pay you a visit the day Melanie disappeared?"

A small gasp escaped Patricia's lips. The unexpected question caught her off guard. She'd been waiting with bated breath for Mallory to press the issue of the leggings, not to turn the conversation so abruptly. Her mind raced as she tried to figure out how best to answer the question without incriminating herself. In retrospect, she should have called a lawyer. Gordon would be furious with her when he found out that she'd talked to Mallory again without counsel. She cleared her throat to buy herself another moment or two to think through her answer. If Tammy had already confessed to visiting her, there was no point in denying it. She would only dig herself in deeper. She smoothed a hand over her sleek bob, puzzling her brow for effect. "Yes, come to think of it, she did stop by. She came over to help me look for Melanie. I was very distressed as you can imagine."

Mallory's eyes drilled into her. "Why did Tammy go to your house? It seems odd that she didn't meet you at the lake where all the other search and rescue volunteers were focusing their efforts to look for your granddaughter."

"Because—" Patricia hesitated. "I ... I was in no state to drive."

Mallory wore a bright smile, but the suspicion in his face was obvious. "Is there anything you want to tell me, Mrs. Galbraith?"

Patricia shrank back from the piercing question. "I ... don't understand, what do you mean?"

He let out an overly patient sigh. "I mean is there anything at all about Melanie's disappearance that you're not telling me?"

Patricia narrowed her eyes at him. "What exactly are you insinuating, sheriff?"

"Nothing. I'm simply asking you to cooperate with this investigation. I can't find your granddaughter if you're hiding things from me."

"I've cooperated to the best of my ability," Patrica replied with a haughty snap of her head. "Perhaps, if you were more competent at your profession, you would have made some progress by now. You're wasting both of our time rehashing what you already know. Why don't you get back out there and start searching for the people who took my grand-daughter before it's too late?"

She glanced up as Brent appeared in the doorway holding aloft a folded piece of paper. He gave Mallory a knowing nod.

Mallory slapped his palms on the table and got to his feet. "Good idea, Mrs. Galbraith. We've got a search warrant for your house, so why don't we start there? I have reason to believe you're concealing evidence in your granddaughter's abduction."

24

*M*allory, Brent and the three additional officers assigned to conduct the search of Patricia Galbraith's home piled through the front door, pulling on disposable gloves, and getting to work without delay. The urgency of finding four-year-old Melanie before it was too late weighed heavily on Mallory. He was stumped by the seemingly contradictory directions the case was taking him in, but more determined than ever to get to the bottom of it. The fact that Patricia Galbraith had failed her polygraph test indicated she knew something about Melanie's abduction, but had she actually perpetrated it, or was she a pawn in someone else's game? If Melanie had been taken by drug dealers Gordon had fallen afoul of, perhaps even owed money to, Patricia's life or her son's might have been threatened for all he knew. Mallory grimaced recalling the satisfied smirk on Tammy's lips as she'd delivered her bombshell news about seeing the pom pom hat hanging on Patricia's coat rack. There was no sign of it here now. Had Tammy been lying about that, like everything else?

"Sir! I think I might have found something," one of the officers called out.

Mallory entered the small room off the kitchen with the French doors which was evidently used as an office. A fresh-faced officer with oversized square glasses sat at the desk, hunched over a laptop. "I've been combing through the search history on Patricia Galbraith's computer," he announced with the jubilant gleam of a pathological gamer in his eye.

Mallory leaned over his shoulder and peered at the screen. "What have you got?"

"Her search history includes a site called missingkids.com, and several other similar sites."

Mallory frowned. "Hardly incriminating. I'd probably have done the same thing if my grandkid had disappeared."

The officer turned to him and pushed his thick glasses up the bridge of his nose. "Uh, three weeks before your grandchild goes missing?"

Mallory straightened up and let out a shocked whistle. "All right, stick with it, I want to know every relevant search she conducted in the past three weeks, also any searches on ransom drops or anything along those lines. Trawl through her emails too. Whatever she was up to, she likely wasn't acting alone."

"On it," the officer replied, his fingers already darting over the keyboard at a speed that defied physics.

Mallory exited the office and went in search of Brent.

One of the other officers directed him to the kitchen just as Brent burst through the door leading from the garage. "Sir!"

Mallory raised his brows questioningly. "What's up?"

"I think you'd better come out here and take a gander for yourself," Brent answered, his voice dropping to a confiding whisper. The look on his face struck fear in Mallory's heart.

"Just tell me we're not too late," he said through gritted teeth.

"I don't honestly know, sir," Brent replied, holding the door open.

With a resigned sigh, Mallory stepped through into a clean and well-organized garage. An officer was busy photographing Patricia Galbraith's Mercedes from every angle while another officer was laying out sealed plastic bags on the ground to be documented and photographed.

Mallory swallowed hard when he caught a glimpse of the miscellaneous purple items inside the bags. He turned to Brent with a sinking feeling. "Do they match what the kid was wearing?"

Brent nodded. "Far as we can tell."

Mallory rubbed his jaw. "Where did you find them?"

"In the trunk of Patricia Galbraith's Mercedes."

MALLORY BRUSHED the side of his nose distractedly as he eyed a tearful Patricia Galbraith from across the table in the same interrogation room they'd sat in earlier that morning. On her right, sat her lawyer with whom she'd had a heated discussion before Mallory had been allowed into the room to conduct his interview. No doubt, the lawyer had not been happy to learn that she'd already talked to Mallory earlier that day.

"Mrs. Galbraith," Mallory began, "We found the clothes your granddaughter was wearing when she disappeared."

Patricia's jaw dropped, shock detonating over her face. "How ... I mean, where?"

"In the trunk of the Mercedes parked in your garage. That is your vehicle, isn't it?"

Patricia opened and closed her mouth several times. She seemed genuinely stunned at the news, scrambling to make sense of it, but Mallory had long since passed the point of trusting any of the Galbraiths' reactions as being legitimate. "Can you explain how Melanie's clothes got there, Mrs. Galbraith?"

"I ... I don't know."

Mallory studied her over his steepled fingers. "Did you have something to do with your granddaughter's disappearance?"

Patricia pressed a hand to the side of her head. "No! I mean ... I didn't abduct Melanie per se," she answered, her voice small and wavering as she struggled to explain herself.

Her lawyer leaned over and whispered something in her ear, but she shook her head and pulled away. "This has gone on long enough. He needs to know the truth."

Mallory fixed as sympathetic a gaze as he could muster on Patricia, sensing she was about to come clean at last. He desperately needed to keep her talking now that she'd started. "What do you mean you didn't abduct Melanie, *per se?*"

Her face crumpled, the words spilling from her lips. "I swear I only wanted to teach Ava a lesson. She's so careless with that child—always getting distracted by her photography. She's been trying to make a case to take Melanie away from Gordon, but she's the negligent one, always has been. That's all I was trying to prove. I wanted Melanie to be with a parent who would watch out for her best interests and make sure nothing bad ever happened to her." Patricia buried her face in a tissue and let out a sharp sob. "Melanie was at my house last Thursday but someone abducted her from there."

Mallory leaned back in his chair, locking eyes with the lawyer as he digested the news. Finally, a breakthrough, although not the one he'd expected. Still, it was better news than he'd anticipated. His fear that one of Gordon's less than desirable business acquaintances had abducted Melanie might prove to be unfounded. Maybe the Galbraiths were simply playing their own twisted game of tug-of-war over the child after all. "Did Gordon know what you were planning to do?"

Patricia shook her head. "He had no idea. Please don't bring him into this. He would never have condoned it if I'd suggested it."

"So let's start at the beginning. How did Melanie end up at your house on Thursday morning?" Mallory asked.

Patricia glanced hesitantly at her lawyer and he nodded for her to continue. "Ava didn't think I knew she was coming up to the lake this weekend, but Gordon had told me a couple of weeks earlier. I knew Ava would go out to photograph the lake in the morning. It wasn't an unusual thing for her to do. She's always out there with her face stuck behind that camera of hers, leaving Melanie unsupervised more often than not." Patricia heaved a sigh and dabbed at her eyes with the soggy tissue.

"And how did you persuade Melanie to accompany you without telling her mother where she was going?" Mallory prodded.

The lawyer frowned at her. "You don't have to answer—"

Patricia leaned across the desk to Mallory, an imploring look on her face. "How I got her to my house is irrelevant. The important thing is that my granddaughter was perfectly safe with me. I admit I wanted to teach Ava a lesson, but that's all there was to it. I had planned to call you and tell you that a friend found Melanie wandering alone on the road, and drove her to my house." She paused, her voice quietening to a whisper. "The real abduction happened afterward. Someone broke into my house and took Melanie. You have to believe me. I had nothing to do with the ransom demand. I would never have done anything to endanger my grand-daughter."

Mallory tapped his foot quietly on the floor beneath the desk. He didn't have to believe anything she said, but his gut told him she was telling the truth for once. "How do you know Melanie didn't leave your house of her own accord to look for her mother?"

Tears slid down Patricia's face. She buried her face in her hands, her shoulders shaking as she fought for composure. After a moment, she looked up again, blinking wet lashes at him. "When she got to my house, I gave her a sleeping pill in her hot chocolate. Enough to knock her out for a few hours." She wrung her hands. "She couldn't possibly have walked out of the house. Somebody must have carried her."

"Do you have any idea who that person might be?"

Patricia tightened her lips, her face constricting with fear. "I've been advised by my lawyer not to say anything more until you grant me immunity from any charges."

Mallory leaned back and scratched his cheek, taken aback at her sudden unwillingness to cooperate just when they were getting somewhere. "I'm not in a position to grant you anything, Mrs. Galbraith. To be honest, it doesn't look particularly good for you right now. As it stands, you're the one who, by your own admission, kidnapped your grand-daughter."

"I didn't *kidnap* my granddaughter," Patricia snapped back indignantly. "I'm allowed to look after her in my own home."

Mallory slung an arm over the back of his chair. "So if you didn't kidnap her, why were the clothes she was wearing when she disappeared hidden in the trunk of your car?"

"Someone planted them there."

Mallory arched a brow. "Who?"

Patricia stared back at him, a defiant gleam in her eye. "The same person who took her from my house."

Mallory straightened up in his seat. "We're going round in circles here. I need a name."

Patricia shot her lawyer a wary look.

Mallory rubbed a hand over his forehead, fighting his mounting frustration as the silence dragged on. "You do realize you could be putting your granddaughter's life in jeopardy by withholding information."

Patricia's lawyer cleared his throat. "My client's prepared to talk in exchange for full immunity from any charges."

Mallory slapped his notebook shut and stood. "Mrs. Galbraith, if what you're telling me is true, your four-year-old granddaughter is in the hands of a kidnapper who is threatening to kill her. *If* she's still alive, it's highly likely she's terrified and confused, crying for her parents, and as it stands, you're the one who's keeping her from them. You think long and hard about what you're doing to Melanie and then we'll talk some more."

25

*M*allory made a few notes in the growing file on the missing child case, before walking into the interview room where Gordon and Ava Galbraith were waiting for him. He had asked Brent to arrange for them to come down to the station and put them in a room together so he could monitor their reactions to one another when they learned what Patricia had confessed to him. He needed to know which of them had taken Melanie from Patricia's house. One or other of her parents must have been responsible for her abduction—it was the only reasonable explanation. There was no sign of forced entry at Patricia's house, and no one other than the Galbraiths had a key. The ransom demand had been a masterful touch to throw him off the trail, but all roads led back to the Galbraiths. Most telling of all was the fact that when Mallory asked Patricia if she had any idea who had abducted her granddaughter, she had gone quiet and refused to say anything more, deferring to her lawyer. The case had gone from one level of bizarre to the next, and he was still no closer to finding the missing four-year-old. He couldn't allow himself to dwell on the possibility that it might already be too late. Both Patricia and her son had the means to spirit Melanie out of the country and make her disappear if that's what it took to keep her from Gordon's estranged wife.

Mallory nodded grimly to Gordon and Ava and then pulled out a chair and sat down opposite them at the conference table. He had resolved to bring them up to speed on what Patricia's search history on her laptop had revealed, but he wasn't planning to tell them that Melanie's clothes had been found in the trunk of her grandmother's car, at least not for now. He needed to be able to eliminate them as co-conspirators first.

Mallory cleared his throat. "Thanks for coming in so promptly. I want to reiterate at the outset that this is a voluntary interview."

"Just get on with it," Gordon snapped, frowning down at his phone when it buzzed. He glanced at the number on the screen before slipping it into his pocket.

Ava threw him a curious glance, but he ignored her.

"As you know, we asked your mother, Patricia, to submit to a polygraph test," Mallory continued, unfazed. "Which I can now confirm she failed."

Gordon's mouth twisted with barely repressed rage. "So you succeeded in terrifying an old woman into hyperventilating and increasing her heart rate. Congratulations! It's an unscientific test and inadmissible in court anyway."

Ignoring the outburst, Mallory flipped open the file on the desk in front of him. "Based on an anonymous tip we received, we secured a search warrant for your mother's home." He paused for effect, his face unsmiling. "You should know that the search history on her laptop included multiple searches on sites about missing kids."

Gordon threw his hands up in the air in exasperation.

"What do you expect a concerned grandparent to do under the circumstances? Online shopping? Give me a break!"

Mallory leaned back in his chair to allow himself a better view to study both Gordon's and Ava's expressions at the same time. "Except that the searches were all conducted in the weeks before Melanie went missing."

Ava blinked rapidly, then frowned, almost as an afterthought.

Not for the first time, her reaction struck Mallory as contrived.

Gordon brushed at an imaginary piece of his fluff on his sleeve, averting his eyes. "Surely you're not suggesting my mother was involved in any way with Melanie's abduction. That makes no sense whatsoever."

Mallory raised a brow, hoping to prompt him to keep talking, and perhaps incriminate himself in the process.

Instead, he scowled back defiantly, as if waiting on Mallory to retract his outrageous allegation.

"I have to agree with Gordon on this," Ava piped up. "Why would Patricia abduct her own granddaughter and then demand a ransom from her son? I realize the note was left for me, but Patricia would have known it was Gordon who would have to come up with the money."

Mallory rubbed a hand over his jaw trying to decide where to take the interview next. Neither Ava nor Gordon had reacted to the news about Patricia's dubious search history with the level of surprise he'd expected, which only reinforced his hunch that they both knew more than they were letting on. But what really struck him as odd was that for once they were in agreement about something. He wondered briefly if one of them had used Patricia's laptop to conduct the searches.

"Patricia claims she didn't send the ransom note," Mallory conceded. "But she did confess to taking Melanie from the lake to her house on Thursday morning and hiding her there for several hours in a misguided attempt to try and bolster Gordon's case for custody. According to her, your daughter was abducted from her house during the course of the morning." He sighed. "There's no sign of forced entry, so that leads us to conclude it was someone with access to the house." He leaned back and waited for the import of his words to take effect.

A solitary muscle twitched in Gordon's face as his eyes bored into Mallory's.

"How do you know Patricia's telling the truth about someone taking Melanie from her house?" Ava said. "Maybe she took her someplace."

"How dare you question my mother!" Gordon yelled, turning to glare at his estranged wife. "You know as well as anyone how much my mother loves Melanie. She wouldn't lie about something like that."

"Wouldn't she?" Ava retorted. "She lied about everything else that happened that morning."

Mallory grimaced. "She does seem genuinely distressed about Melanie's disappearance. Apparently, her plan was to call me after a couple of hours and report that someone found Melanie wandering unaccompanied and drove her to her place. She also confessed to drugging her with sleeping medication in her hot chocolate so there's no way Melanie could have walked out of her house. Someone must have carried her out."

"Did she say who drove Melanie from the lake to her house?" Gordon demanded. "Evidently, she had help."

Now it was Mallory's turn to avert his eyes. He could swear by the unsettling look Gordon gave him that he knew the answer to his question already, and the thought shook Mallory to his core. Had Tammy helped Patricia kidnap Melanie?

Ava raised her brows questioningly and Mallory tried not to squirm under her equally intense gaze. Maybe they both knew what had happened to Melanie, and they were testing him. All of a sudden, he felt like he was the one being interrogated. Sweat prickled along his hairline. "We're looking into it. Mrs. Galbraith's not cooperating at the moment." He paused. "I need to ask if either of you wish to press charges against her?"

"Absolutely not!" Gordon spat out. "My wife's the one you should be pressing charges against. It was her negligence that allowed this to happen in the first place."

Mallory looked at Ava. "You can still press charges against your mother-in-law if you wish, although you should be aware that your own actions will also come under scrutiny. Child Protection Services may be called upon to do an evaluation."

"I don't wish to press any charges," Ava said emphatically. "I just want you to find my daughter."

Mallory gave a curt nod and closed the file in front of him. "Then you're both free to go, for now. Please make sure you're available for further questioning as needed. The FBI will be here tomorrow to assist us with the case. In the meantime, search and rescue will continue working around the clock to locate your daughter."

Mallory observed silently as Gordon and Ava got to their feet and exchanged wary glances. The charged atmosphere between them was palpable. It was a stretch to think they could have conspired with one another in their own daughter's abduction from her grandmother's house. They harbored too much hostility toward each other to collaborate on anything. But for the life of him Mallory was still no clearer on which of them had been behind it. He needed to talk to Hal and see if he'd managed to dig up anything else on Melanie's parents. He flipped the file on the table closed and stood. "If either of you need a ride, one of my officers will be happy to drive you."

Gordon threw Ava a sharp glance. "I'm not going back to the cabin. I'm headed to my mother's place."

"In that case, I'll take a ride from one of the officers," Ava said.

Mallory nodded and turned to address Gordon. "If you're not planning on staying at the cabin tonight, I'm afraid you'll have to book into a hotel for the night and text me the address in case we need to reach you. Your mother's house is a potential crime scene so you won't be able to access it other than to collect your personal items, under supervision naturally."

Gordon stomped over to the door and yanked it open. "Believe me, Mallory, by the time my lawyers are done with you, you won't be going anywhere ever again without supervision."

26

Tammy lifted her car keys from the rack on the kitchen wall and slung her purse over her shoulder. There was no way she could get the funds together that Jeremy had demanded, but she wouldn't need to. She had a plan of her own to make sure he didn't make any demands of her ever again. He had turned out to be a huge disappointment, a weight dragging her down that she had tolerated for far too long. If he hadn't shared a prison cell with her father —and got his stamp of approval—she'd never have given him a chance to begin with.

Just as she reached out to open the door to the garage, her phone rang. Glancing down she saw Gordon's number flash onto the screen. She gritted her teeth. She wasn't ready to talk to him yet. If he still thought she was behind the ransom demand, he'd want his money back, as well as his daughter, and she had neither. She hesitated, debating whether or not to take the call. It might work in her favor if she could manage to delay him. And she needed all the time she could get to complete her plan to get rid of any evidence that might lead back to her. Her mind made up, she walked back to the kitchen table, set down her purse and keys, and swiped her finger across the screen. "Hello, darling. So good to hear from you again."

"I want my daughter, Tammy. I know you took her. You got the money you wanted. I swear I'm coming over there and putting a bullet in your head if you don't tell me where she is right this minute."

Tammy inhaled a deep breath. He was worked up but he didn't mean what he was saying. Gordon couldn't live without her. And she couldn't live without him. They needed each other in a primal sort of way that superseded everything and everyone around them. She just had to remind him of that fact. She would even get his wretched child back if that's what he wanted—if that's what it would take to bring him back to her. But first, she needed a commitment from him.

She tinkled an amused laugh. "Calm down, Gordon, you're all bent out of shape about something I had absolutely no control over. This was all your mother's idea. You know how obsessive she can be. She came to me in tears, begging me to help. She was the one—"

"You set my mother up so you could get your hands on my daughter!"

"I merely gave her some advice—"

"Where ... is ... Melanie?" Gordon screamed into the phone.

Tammy squeezed her eyes shut. "All right, all right. Listen to me. I admit I took it one step further. But only because I wanted to help you. I wanted to make perfectly sure that Ava had no chance of getting custody. Your mother and I both did what we did for you. You know how much I love you, Gordon. We belong together, we always have."

"What exactly *did* you do, Tammy?"

She flinched as his words rasped over her like fingernails.

Gordon's voice was so cold she could almost imagine him shivering with rage. In a strange kind of way, it excited her to think about the passion pumping through him, his attention in this moment fully fixed on her—the way she liked it. They were so good together it hurt in the best kind of way.

"I hired Jeremy Ward to take Melanie from your mother's house," she said. "I left the window in the guest bedroom unlatched so he could get in. He was only supposed to keep her overnight at his parents' place." The lie slipped like butter from her lips. She wasn't about to admit to Gordon that she'd hired someone to do away with his daughter to punish him for leaving her. He need never know how far she'd taken it. "It was Jeremy's idea to demand the ransom," she went on. "He got greedy. But that's the downside of conducting business with the criminal element. You never know what—"

"Where … is … she?" Gordon demanded. Tammy arched a brow, relishing the ardor in his voice. Mallory never talked to her like that. His tone was usually somewhere between despondent or apologetic when he addressed her, both of which she despised. It had been a bitter disappointment to discover that the giant of a man she'd married was so soft on the inside. It nauseated her. Tammy pressed her lips to the back of her hand and studied the pink imprint her gloss left behind. Such a shame that Gordon had tried to end their relationship. He'd forced her to punish him like this. She could have helped him get custody of Melanie. She could even have become the kid's mother with Ava out of the way. But Gordon had rejected her, and if he didn't want Tammy, he wasn't going to have Melanie either. "I'm on my way to pick her up right now, darling. Jeremy got the ransom and he asked me to fetch Melanie. He didn't want to risk leaving her somewhere on her own and sending you the coordinates in case something happened to her."

"I'm coming with you."

"No!" Tammy gripped the edge of the kitchen table, her fingernails digging into the wood. "He won't show up if you do. Trust me. If I don't go alone to the rendezvous point, he won't turn her over. He's not going to risk going back to jail for kidnapping and extortion. You can't expect him to trust you after what you did to him."

"Why should I believe you?" Gordon fumed. "How do I know Jeremy Ward's even involved in this? I'm beginning to think you set the whole thing up to ruin me financially as a punishment for breaking things off. You just can't accept that it's over between us."

Tammy threw back her head and laughed. "Darling! You have such a vivid imagination lurking in that cold, calculating brain of yours. No wonder I love you to pieces. It's your mind I lust after, not your money. I'm not in the business of conducting illicit activities involving large sums of cash, Gordon. I think we both know who's better at that, and I'm sure my husband would be very interested to hear all about your dealings."

A long silence ensued before Gordon responded. "If you don't bring my daughter back today, I swear you're going down for this. You know I have people who can dispose of you so well that Mallory won't even have a bone fragment left to bury. You have until 6.00 pm tonight. I'm at a hotel. I'll text you my address."

"Such a threatening tone, darling, you do know what that does to me, don't you?"

Tammy smirked when the line went dead. She was thoroughly enjoying feeling Gordon squirm under her newfound power over him.

*G*ordon paced the floor of his room at the Lake View Inn as he waited for Tammy's call confirming that she had picked up Melanie. She should have been in touch by now, but he'd heard nothing and she wasn't responding to any of his texts or calls. In the meantime, he was forced to wait in this fleabag hotel until she deigned to call him, while his lawyers worked on hammering out an immunity deal for his mother. Mallory had refused to allow Gordon to talk to her until the deal was signed which infuriated him. He had a hunch Mallory was doing some digging into his business affairs while trying to keep him in the dark about the fact that he was being investigated. But Gordon wasn't afraid of Mallory or his crew of inept officers uncovering anything incriminating that they could make stick. Gordon had invested more than enough time, money and effort to make sure any trails they stumbled onto would grow cold before they led anywhere. He gave a hard laugh as he undid his tie and tossed it on the bed. If only Mallory knew who was really behind Melanie's abduction. All in good time. He wouldn't nail Tammy until he was sure Melanie was safe. Tammy was too unpredictable.

He still couldn't comprehend what had possessed his mother to do what she had done. Then again, Tammy Anderson could be very persuasive. He was living proof of that. He had attempted countless times over the years to end their relationship, but somehow she always coaxed him into returning to her lair. She wielded that kind of power over him—she was exhilarating in a way no other woman was, least of all Ava.

Gordon checked his phone again as though a message might have surreptitiously found its way onto the device. Anger flared up inside him. Why wasn't she responding? He still wasn't sure if Tammy had acted alone or actually enlisted Jeremy as an accomplice to abduct Melanie from his mother's house. The thought sent a wave of panic through him. Jeremy Ward had an axe to grind with Gordon that made him extremely dangerous. If it turned out Tammy had left Melanie alone with him, he would make sure she paid for it. Once Melanie was safe, he would make it his priority to get rid of Tammy, along with that pompous consolation prize of a sheriff she'd married when Gordon had dumped her the first time around.

He glanced at his screen for the umpteenth time but there was still no communication from Tammy. He set down his mobile on the bedside table and walked over to the mini bar. He could use a stiff drink to take the edge off. After selecting a Jack Daniels, he added a few ice cubes to a glass and downed the drink in one gulp. The buzz only heightened his frustration. He should have listened to his mother and made a clean break with Tammy years ago. Trouble was, she got him in a way that no one else did. He could be his provocative, ruthless self around her and it only made him all the more attractive to her. It was part of her appeal—her desire to live dangerously. And he had to admit that Tammy was still an exceptionally gorgeous woman who took excellent care of herself, unlike Ava who, despite the generous allowance he provided her with, seemed content to parade around looking like a hippie photographer. Gordon plucked an ice cube from his glass and sucked on it. He hadn't been able to keep away from Tammy all these years because he hadn't wanted to. Now, he was paying the price for his weakness.

He grimaced when he thought of everything his mother was currently going through thanks to Tammy's toxic scheming. Although he had an excellent team of expensive lawyers on board to ensure his mother walked away from this mess, the strain of being treated like a criminal would not be easy for a woman like Patricia Galbraith who prided herself on her status in the community. Thankfully, albeit for reasons he didn't understand, Ava hadn't been interested in pressing charges against his mother. He had no doubt the lawyers would get her name fully cleared once she agreed to testify against Tammy. It wouldn't be hard to convince the judge that a loving grandmother had been manipulated by a conniving police officer's wife who was also a scorned lover. Gordon brushed a stray thread from his pant leg. It was regrettable that his affair with Tammy would inevitably become public knowledge, but it was the cost of getting his daughter back.

His reputation would take a hit, but he had no intention of returning to Brooksbury after this so it wouldn't matter in the long run. The last of the boxes were due to be moved from the cabin and into his new warehouse tomorrow night. In the last few years, his business had expanded beyond his wildest dreams. Ava could keep the house in Cedarville for all he cared. Once the divorce was finalized, he would purchase a new gated property with a secondary residence and set his mother up in the guest house where she would be free to see Melanie as often as she wanted. He wasn't concerned about Ava thwarting his plans, she was a much less complex loose end to take care of than Tammy. Ava had neither the backbone nor the brains to take him on, in or out of court. After this regrettable incident, he had no doubt she would lose custody of Melanie. He had paid his lawyers handsomely to make sure of it. And his pockets ran a whole lot deeper than Ava suspected.

Granted, he had taken a few risks early on conducting some business transactions in Brooksbury where everyone knew him, but the small town loser sheriff, Mallory, remained oblivious, and the remote location of the cabin had proved a perfect hideaway. Jeremy Ward had been a useful accomplice when he'd first started money laundering for drug dealers, until Jeremy had gotten greedy. Gordon had had no choice but to set him up in order to get rid of him. Jeremy had kept his mouth shut in prison after Gordon warned him that he would mail his parents' ashes to his cell if he squealed.

His phone chimed letting him know he had an incoming text message. He snatched it up and stared at the screen, willing it to be Tammy confirming she was bringing Melanie to his hotel room. As he read the words, his pulse began a dull thud that had nothing to do with the alcohol seeping through his veins. He tapped on the message app to open it up and read the text in full.

Hello Gordon. I'm going to offer you one last opportunity to retrieve your daughter. Bring the five-hundred-thousand dollars to the following coordinates at midnight. 38.5195° N, 121.3827° W. Wait inside the hunting cabin with the money. Come alone and unarmed. Do not inform the police. If you deviate from these instructions a second time, the next set of coordinates you receive will be for your daughter's remains.

Gordon swore loudly. He picked up his glass and hurled it across the room, roaring with frustration as it shattered. He didn't recognize the number, but he had no doubt this was Tammy's handiwork. Either she owned a second phone or she was in cahoots with Jeremy Ward as she had claimed. He didn't doubt for a minute that Jeremy would jump at the chance to get his revenge. Had he demanded more money or had Tammy put him up to this? Maybe they'd agreed to split the funds. No wonder she'd been adamant that he wait behind. He should have insisted on going with her to pick up Melanie.

Gordon frowned and scrubbed a hand over his jaw. Tammy was still as obsessed with him as ever. Surely she wasn't trying to double-cross him after confessing to what she had done and practically pleading with him to get back together with her. The more he thought about it, the more likely it seemed that Jeremy had put her up to this—threatened her perhaps. But, if Jeremy thought he could bleed him dry, he had another thing coming. There was no way he was getting another half-a-million out of him. One way or another, Gordon would end this tonight and bring his daughter home.

He rubbed his fingertips across his brow, rereading the text as as he plotted his next move. He would show up at the cabin, alone, as the note stipulated, but not unarmed. In fact, he would be waiting for Jeremy long before midnight with a very special kind of greeting. After that, he would figure out how to get rid of Tammy. He picked up his phone and dialed. First, he would need some supplies.

GORDON LAID the suitcase that had been delivered to his room on the bed and opened it up. He took his time selecting what he would need to carry on his person, before locking the case back up again and departing his room shortly before 11.00pm. Once he had loaded the suitcase into his car, he plugged in the coordinates from the text, before backing out of his parking spot outside his room at the Lake View Inn.

Adrenalin pumped in his veins as he drove away. Tammy had more brains than most people he knew, but she'd overestimated her ability pitting her wits against him, and recruiting Jeremy Ward to help her. No one got the better of Gordon Galbraith. Tammy had always been a con artist, she'd grown up learning the ropes from her father, but Gordon had developed into quite the accomplished conman himself over the years. It was time to show her what he was capable of. Unfortunately for Jeremy Ward, he would be the one taking the fall again, a fitting response to his betrayal. Gordon grinned to himself. The gun Jeremy had wielded in the botched heist that had put him behind bars the first time lay nestled in the case on the back seat.

When Gordon reached the turnoff that led to the forest service road the coordinates guided him to, he slowed to a crawl and pulled on a black ski mask. He didn't anticipate any problems, but if this didn't go as planned he couldn't risk anyone identifying him afterward. He could have called in someone to do the job for him, but he wanted to handle it himself. Tammy had made it personal. The good times between them were over—she had become too dangerous a diversion to keep around any longer. She already knew too much about his operation, and now that she'd paired up with Jeremy Ward, he was willing to bet she knew a whole lot more. Still, if he could persuade her to move south of the border on a permanent basis, they might be able to come to some sort of arrangement. A nice compound, her own bodyguards, a generous allowance. She was right about how good they were together. It would be a shame not to at least leave the door open.

He shifted into four-wheel drive and drove along the rutted snow-covered road that followed the river for close to two miles before he spotted a good place to hide his vehicle from prying eyes. The remainder of the trek would have to be made on foot. He pulled off the road and turned left down toward the river into an isolated camping spot shielded from the road by a dense growth of pine trees.

After retrieving the rest of the items from the case he'd brought with him, he locked his car and took off at a brisk march toward the hunting cabin. According to his GPS it was another quarter mile up a moderately steep trail. The fungal scent of the forest blended with the distinctive scent of pine as he began to climb, shining his flashlight in front of him to light his way. Gnarled roots zig-zagged across the trail beneath the snow, hampering his ascent and forcing him to slow his pace. The equipment he was carrying was heavier than he'd anticipated. His ragged breathing etched through the night, branches creaking and swaying around him in the cool breeze that swept through the forest.

At last the path leveled out and the hunting cabin came into view. Gordon slipped behind a large tree trunk and scoped out his surroundings looking for the ideal location to set up—someplace with a clear view of the trail, but providing plenty of cover. Once he'd found the perfect vantage point, he settled in to wait for his quarry to arrive. He wouldn't take Jeremy out if he had Melanie with him. He had no desire to traumatize his daughter any more than she already had been. In that case, he would wait to make sure there was no one following them, and then approach the cabin. As soon as his daughter was safe, he would take care of business.

Of course, if Jeremy pulled a weapon on him and refused to turn over Melanie, he would have no option but to take him out there and then, in full view of his daughter—not his first choice but it came with the territory. He couldn't protect Melanie twenty-four hours a day, and the increasingly lucrative deals he was making were growing inherently more risky. After this was all over, he would hire a personal bodyguard for Melanie. No one, man, woman, or ex-wife, was ever going to put his daughter in harm's way again.

28

---

*M*allory returned to the interview room where Patricia Galbraith waited with her lawyer. He fought to keep his expression neutral as he nodded a greeting to them. In light of the fact that neither Gordon nor Ava wanted to press charges, he had little choice but to grant her request for immunity in order to get the information he so desperately needed. It troubled him that none of the Galbraiths demonstrated the same sense of urgency to find Melanie and bring her home as he did—an observation that only confirmed for him that they knew where she was and were for some incomprehensible reason keeping the information from him. He sat down at the table and pulled out his notebook. "Mrs. Galbraith, we're prepared to grant you immunity from prosecution if you agree to cooperate fully with the ongoing investigation from this point forward."

Her lawyer's nostrils twitched like he was sniffing something unpalatable. "We'll need both testimonial and transactional immunity or the deal is off."

Mallory inclined his head in acknowledgement and slid a sheet of paper his way. "Here you go. It's all been drawn up."

The lawyer perused the terms of the deal briefly before turning to Patricia. "This looks to be in order. You can sign it. Go ahead and answer the sheriff's questions to the best of your ability, unless I advise you otherwise."

Mallory sat back in his chair and waited for Patricia to set down her pen. Adopting his most patient tone, he began, "Mrs. Galbraith, I'd like to go back to where we left off earlier. How exactly did you persuade Melanie to accompany you from the lake to your house without telling her mother where she was going?"

Patricia eyed him coolly. Her whole demeanor had changed now that she had secured immunity. "I hired someone to do the job for me."

Mallory raised a brow. "So Melanie's abduction was hardly a spontaneous act."

"Irrelevant," Patricia's lawyer piped up. "We're not trying to prosecute Mrs. Galbraith. That's off the table now." He leaned over and whispered something to her and she nodded in agreement.

Mallory took a few notes and then continued, "Ava said she didn't see any clear prints next to Melanie's footprints. Can you explain that?"

Patricia shrugged. "I wasn't there to witness how it went down."

Mallory gave her an appraising glance. "Did you come up with the idea yourself to abduct your granddaughter or did someone help you plan it?"

Patricia shot her lawyer a questioning look before answering, "Someone suggested it to me as a way to ensure Gordon would get custody. I was dubious at first, but they were very convincing. They planned the whole thing, and then abducted Melanie and brought her to my house."

Mallory's heart lurched in his chest as he began to make an uncomfortable connection. He concentrated on his notes for a moment before meeting Patricia's disdainful gaze that seemed to be begging the question he forced through his lips, "And who was that person?"

"It was your wife of course, sheriff." Patricia pressed her lips together tightly before adding in a scathing tone. "But I think you already know that."

Her lawyer muttered something in her ear but she merely let out an irritated humph before continuing. "Tammy and Gordon were having an affair on and off for years, a fact I was not aware of until yesterday. Gordon told me he broke it off for good a couple of weeks ago but Tammy wasn't having any part of it. She hounded him constantly—texting and calling—but he wouldn't relent." Patricia tucked a few strands of her silver bob carefully behind one ear. "Tammy came up with this whole scheme to punish my son for dumping her. She ingratiated herself with me so she could convince me to participate in it. She said it would make Ava look like a negligent mother and bolster Gordon's case to gain full custody. I was foolish enough to believe her."

Mallory could feel the pulse in his temples hammering like a war drum. He fought to stay composed, plowing on with his line of questioning even as his vision blurred. The affair with Gordon was treacherous enough, but plotting to kidnap a four-year-old child to punish him was another thing entirely. "That's a very serious allegation you're making against my wife," he heard himself say. "Do you have any evidence to support your claim?"

Patricia rummaged in her purse for her phone and placed it on the table between them. She curved her lips into a cool smile. "All the evidence is there. You're welcome to read through it for yourself, but then again, I suspect you've seen it before."

Mallory frowned, his eyes flicking briefly to the lawyer's.

Not for the first time in this investigation, he felt like he was the accused, his wife's guilt weighing him down like a wet blanket over his shoulders that he couldn't shrug off. He needed to know just how far she'd gone—had she been the one who'd demanded the ransom and threatened to kill Melanie? He reached for Patricia's phone, trying to mask the tremor in his hand, and placed it inside an evidence bag before addressing her again. "Earlier, you said that the clothes Melanie was wearing when she disappeared were planted in your car by the person who abducted her from your house later that day. Do you know who that person was?"

"Tammy, of course," Patricia snapped, her eyes slits of hatred as she spat out the words. "Who else?"

Mallory maintained a careful air of calm, despite the thundering waterfall of emotions inside his chest. "Can you prove that?"

Anger rippled across Patricia's face. "You don't have to be a detective to connect the dots. She made up the bed in the guest room while I got Melanie's hot chocolate ready. She was the only one who had an opportunity to unlatch the window. And when she came back over to my house later on pretending to help me look for Melanie, she grabbed her snow clothes from the rack in the hall and said she'd get rid of them for me. She made a point of leaving the house through the garage so no one would spot her with Melanie's clothes. She must have planted them in my car on her way out." Patricia stared coldly at Mallory. "I guess it wasn't enough to punish Gordon, she wanted revenge on me too. She still blames me for taking Gordon away from her all those years ago."

Mallory grimaced as he took a few more notes. He had to admit that Patricia's analysis of his wife's motives made perfect sense. "Is it possible a third person was involved in

Melanie's abduction? Did you or Tammy involve anyone else in your scheme?"

Patricia wrapped her arms around herself. "I wasn't involved in any scheme. I was simply trying to do what I thought was in the best interests of my granddaughter. She would have been perfectly safe at my house for a few hours. It was Tammy who had the scheme going—all the lies she fed me, stringing Gordon along for all those years, the ransom demand. Her greed and deception know no bounds." She rose half-way out of her seat, her voice rising. "It's your own wife you should be talking to! Ask *her* if she had an accomplice! She's the one who's holding my granddaughter! That woman is psychotic. You have no idea what she's capable of."

Her lawyer laid a restraining hand on her arm and she sank back down in her seat, her body twitching with rage.

Mallory got to his feet, stone-faced. Patricia was right. He had no idea what his wife was capable of, but after everything he'd learned in the past few hours, he feared the worst. "Thank you for your cooperation, Mrs. Galbraith," he said, lacing his words with an edge of cynicism. "Let's just hope for your sake it didn't come too late to save your granddaughter."

29

*T*ammy reached for her car keys lying where she'd tossed them on her kitchen table. She pictured Gordon growing increasingly restless in his hotel room as his arbitrary deadline demanding his daughter's safe return came and went. A small smile of satisfaction formed on her lips. She needed to let him suffer a little for what he had done to her. In fact, he deserved to suffer a lot. And there was really only one way to ensure that happened, only one fool-proof way to rip out his heart like he'd ripped out hers. She tapped her fingernails irritably on the table. Jeremy had failed her on that point, wanting more and more money to take care of business. Then, he'd come up with the hare-brained idea of demanding an exorbitant ransom for Melanie's safe return. She'd underestimated his stupidity. Now the FBI were involved. They would be here in the morning to take over the investigation from Mallory—but they would arrive too late to foil her plans. By then, there wouldn't be any need for their hostage negotiating services. Come tomorrow, Melanie would no longer be a missing person. But Jeremy Ward would be. And a decades long manhunt for a child killer would begin. Tammy let out a huff of amusement. Jeremy would never be found. She would make sure of it.

Minutes later, she backed out of her driveway and drove across town to her mother's trailer. Most Saturday nights, her mother went to bingo at the community hall and slept over at her sister's, which made it all the easier for Tammy to look for what she needed without having to explain herself. As expected, no one answered when she rapped her knuckles on the door. She went around to the back of the trailer and retrieved a key from beneath a blue ceramic flower pot filled with a dead ball of roots belonging to an unidentifiable plant from a bygone era. After letting herself in, she checked to make sure her mother wasn't napping on the sagging couch before making her way to the tiny bedroom at the back of the trailer. She lifted up the mattress and rummaged through the clothing and blankets in the storage area beneath until she found the bag she was looking for. Her gun was still inside, and loaded. It had amused her no end when Mallory had insisted on sending her to the gun range to learn how to defend herself after they got married, even gifting her with a Glock of her own. Little did he know, she'd owned and operated a gun long before she married him, one that couldn't be traced back to her. Her father hadn't been good for much when he'd been alive, but at least he'd taught her a few tricks of the trade that had proven worthwhile.

She carried the bag back up to the main living space and set it down on the floor while she retrieved some old newspapers from the pile next to the couch. Scrunching up a handful of sheets into balls, she began stuffing the bag, throwing in an overdue library book she found wedged in the couch to add some weight. The bag would only have to serve as a momentary distraction—she would pass it off as the additional money Jeremy had demanded. If things went as planned, he would never lay a hand on it. Once he was out of the way, she'd retrieve what she could of the money she'd already given him, and possibly even the ransom money. She had a sneaking suspicion he'd been winding her up about not receiving it. Gordon would never have risked his daughter's life by failing to deliver the money.

Tammy stashed the bag in her car and then came back inside and poured herself a glass of Sauvignon Blanc from an open bottle in the tiny refrigerator. She might as well pass the evening at her mother's trailer and avoid the possibility of running into Mallory if he came home at some point to pick up a change of clothes. He was closing in on her, and she needed to wrap things up before she left him for good. Thanks to Gordon's contacts, she would be able to vanish without a trace—well, almost. She wanted Gordon to find her—to come crawling back to her once he remembered she was the center of his world. Tammy hummed to herself as she fished out her phone to text Mallory and tell him she was going out for drinks and spending the night at a friend's.

Shortly after eleven, she climbed into her car and plugged in the coordinates Jeremy had sent her. The night air was dry and bitterly cold and she cranked up the heater, teeth chattering, as she pulled out of the trailer park and drove west toward the mountains. She turned onto a potholed forest road and followed it for a couple of bone-shaking miles, slowing down as she approached the steep trail the coordinates were leading her to. It wouldn't do to leave her car out in the open, she'd have to find somewhere remote to park where it wouldn't be spotted. She kept driving for a few more minutes until the forest service road petered out in a dead end, and then pulled her car behind a copse of towering pine trees. Grabbing the bag and a flashlight, she retraced her steps to the bottom of the trail.

Sucking in a steadying breath, Tammy began making her

way cautiously up the side of the hill through the trees staked out like charcoal sentries. Her hand rested on the gun inside the cheap, plastic bag that bumped against her hip as she walked. An owl swooped down from the trees to her left letting out a spine-tingling screech as it latched onto a kill, before retreating with its quarry. Tammy watched the whole episode impassively. The air felt right for killing.

Snow crunched beneath her boots, glistening in the moonlight that spilled a gauzy shaft of light into the forest. Tammy smirked, picturing an inconsolable Ava Galbraith crying herself to sleep at night after Melanie's body was discovered. Ava's loss was entirely her own fault—she had made it all so incredibly easy. Too engrossed in her photography to keep track of her insufferable offspring. But, as Gordon often said, she had a pancake for a brain and it had been flipped one time too many. Ava had never really been the threat, it was Melanie who had stolen the spotlight, and Gordon's affection. It was time to make things right between them again. Once Tammy took care of business, she would be waiting in the wings to comfort Gordon in his loss. He would need her then more than ever.

It had been Tammy's idea to spy on Ava and Melanie with her binoculars while they were out early at the lake taking pictures last Thursday morning. And it had been Tammy's idea to cover her ultralight snowshoes with pillowcases, and carry Melanie over to Patricia's waiting Mercedes, which she had proceeded to roll down the road until she was far enough out of earshot to start it without being heard. Tammy curled her lip in disgust when Patricia's pinched face came to mind. Too bad she wouldn't have enough time to get rid of Gordon's mother too. It had been tedious pretending to befriend her. The woman was beyond cringeworthy—utterly dependent on her son for everything, with scarcely an independent thought. *Gordon says this... Gordon says that...* No wonder she'd favored Ava over Tammy as the more suitable bride for her precious boy—Ava was the perfect puppy to train. Compliant and weak.

Tammy hadn't needed Gordon the way the other women in his life did. That was the reason he couldn't keep away from her. But, he had deeply disappointed her and he would have to pay for his sins.

30

*A*t eleven-thirty, Gordon heard what sounded like a footfall. He stilled his breathing and listened intently trying to determine if it was human, or simply an animal moving through the brush. He wasn't much of a hunter—he'd never enjoyed it on the few occasions he'd been out with Jeremy Ward. All that squatting in the dirt, the insect bites, the cold, the heat, the dark, the crappy coffee. He'd only gone with Jeremy to cement his loyalty early on when he was still building up his business. But, this was a different kind of hunt. This engendered the kind of thrill that made every physical discomfort pale in comparison, the kind of thrill that warmed Gordon's blood the way only Tammy ordinarily could.

After a moment or two, he made out the definite sound of someone tromping through the brush in the direction of the cabin. He grimaced. Jeremy had arrived earlier than he'd anticipated. He lined up his scope and waited, one shallow breath away from a kill shot. A moment later, a dark figure came into view—no sign of Melanie in tow. Through his night vision goggles, Gordon could just about make out the features of Tammy's face as she slipped behind a tree and peered in the direction of the cabin. He clenched his jaw and lowered his rifle, reeling from shock. So he had been right all along—Tammy was the one behind the ransom demands. He had to admire her nerve. All that talk of Jeremy Ward had only been a ruse to throw him off her trail. It was time he got rid of her, once and for all, before his weakness became his undoing.

He raised his gun again and took aim. A fleeting moment of doubt worked its way into his thoughts. Was this really what he wanted—to put an end to his nemesis? His mind was in a quandary even now, resolved as he had been a moment ago to go through with it. Tammy was like an addiction that he wanted to quash and simultaneously drink from past the point of intoxication. Maybe he didn't actually have to go as far as killing her. He could punish her instead. He could force her to turn over Melanie and then have her prosecuted for child abduction and extortion. On his mother's testimony, Tammy would go to prison for a long time and Mallory would lose everything he had stolen from Gordon all those years ago. A grin crept over Gordon's lips. A double-edged strike that would give him a certain level of satisfaction. After all, he'd still be able to visit Tammy in prison if he found he simply couldn't stay away.

But then he remembered Melanie's soft, chestnut curls brushing against his face when she kissed him, the sweet smell of her skin, the dimples in her creamy cheeks when she smiled, and his resolve hardened. Tammy had crossed a line no one had the right to cross.

He took a few deep breaths, frowning in concentration. Patience was required to make sure that nothing went awry. He would blow out her kneecap first and then force her to tell him where she was holding Melanie before he finished her off.

As his finger tightened around the trigger, a twig snapped somewhere off to his left. He froze, turning his head ever so slowly in that direction. Was someone else here? Had Tammy arranged for Jeremy to bring Melanie to the cabin? Tammy might have promised to divide the ransom money straight down the line in return for Jeremy's assistance—a promise Gordon knew she would renege on the first chance she got. But Jeremy Ward was too stupid to see it coming.

Gordon remained motionless. He didn't dare give away his position by shooting Tammy now. Jeremy Ward might not have won the cerebral jackpot, but he was an excellent marksman. Gordon wasn't about to risk taking a bullet to the back of his own head if Jeremy was staked out somewhere just out of sight. Had he been here all along, or had he crept up on the cabin unbeknownst to Gordon?

After a few tense moments, a solitary deer appeared between the trees, chewing on some stems peeking through the snow as it moved nonchalantly through the forest. Gordon relaxed his cramped muscles and let out a long, silent breath before turning his attention back to Tammy. His eyes darted left and right searching in vain for her shadow. He swore under his breath. She must have already slipped inside the hunting cabin. He would have to move on to plan B.

After waiting for several more minutes to make sure the coast was clear, Gordon climbed out of his mossy hideout and stole silently toward the cabin, keeping a wary eye out over his shoulder for any movement in the undergrowth behind him, listening for the sound of a footfall coming up the trail. Jeremy could still show up at any minute. He might even be inside the hut holding Melanie hostage until the money exchanged hands. Gordon gritted his teeth. If that turned out to be the case, it added a layer of complication to his plan. But he had come prepared for all eventualities. He wasn't leaving here tonight without his daughter.

*T*ammy was panting hard by the time the steep trail leveled out and the shadowy form of the hunting cabin loomed in front of her. From behind a large oak tree, she watched and waited for a moment or two to make sure there was no indication that Jeremy had arrived ahead of her. She wondered if he would bring Melanie with him or if he would want to pick up his money before he turned over his hostage. Tammy suppressed a tiny snort of laughter at the irony of it. If Jeremy was holding Melanie at some undisclosed location, she might never be found. After all, Jeremy wasn't going to be leaving here alive tonight.

Satisfied that there was no sign of life at the cabin, Tammy switched off her flashlight and made her way quietly toward the dilapidated wooden building. With as light a touch as possible, she pushed open the front door on its reluctant hinges and peered cautiously around the interior, relieved to find it empty except for a few shadowy pieces of ramshackle furniture. She had arrived early with the express purpose of setting up an ambush. Jeremy was a loose cannon, proving more difficult to control than she had anticipated. He had gone too far with his ransom demands and blackmail. And now that he had begun, he might never stop. It was imperative she got rid of him before he squealed or bled her dry.

Gordon's daughter was another matter entirely. If she could find her, Melanie might still have her uses. Tammy was oscillating back and forth between finishing her off or bringing her back like a tribute to Gordon. It might go a long way to restoring their relationship if she played Melanie's savior, but if she was being honest with herself she was tired of playing second fiddle to the child. She'd much rather see Gordon broken, and craving the kind of comfort that only she could give him.

A rustling sound outside the cabin caught her attention, shocking her out of her reverie. She took a couple of shallow breaths, her senses on high alert. Jeremy had arrived early too. She shivered, berating herself for not staying more focused on the task at hand. The man could blend into his surroundings for hours on end without flinching a muscle. It was possible he'd watched her approach to make sure she had come alone, as instructed. She placed the black bag on the cobwebbed table in full view of anyone entering the cabin, and then hunkered down behind the door to wait. Pulling out her gun, she quickly chambered a round and waited for the door to scrape open. She was confident Jeremy's eyes would immediately be drawn to the decoy bag on the table in front of him. Satisfying his greed had always been his first priority, as long as she'd known him. In the split second it took for his eyes to flick to the bag, she would put a bullet in his skull and end this.

Seconds ticked by and then Tammy heard a scuffling sound outside on the porch. Slowly, the door began to creak inward. She held her breath for an elongated moment, and then took aim as a dark figure stepped through and waved the barrel of a gun in a single sweep around the room. She shot once through the back of the head, both hands holding her own weapon steady, clean and committed like her father had taught her. The figure dropped with a dull, satisfying thud on the wooden floor.

Her arms relaxed as she let out the breath she had been holding. She got to her feet, gun still aimed at the prostrate body. With a contemptuous kick of her boot, she confirmed he was dead. Satisfied, she lowered her gun, stuffed it into the back of her waistband and knelt at his side. "You shouldn't have double-crossed me, Ward. I trained you better than that. Too bad it turned out you weren't in my league after all." She reached out and yanked the ski mask from his head.

Her eyes widened in horror, a cold iron stake bearing through her ribs and piercing her heart. Her grip on her gun went slack and she let it slide to the floor with a clatter. *No! It can't be!* Her mind ran in confused circles as she tried to grasp the shadowy reality of what she was seeing. Gordon lay dead on the floor in front of her, blood oozing from his head. It made no sense. What was he doing here? "Gordon!" she screamed. "Gordon, can you hear me?"

She slipped a shaking hand beneath his neck and tried to raise his bloodied head into her lap. Her mind reeled, trying to piece together how this could have happened, how she could have made such a terrible mistake. It should be Jeremy lying here in a pool of blood—not her beloved Gordon, slain by her own hand. Jeremy was supposed to be meeting her here at midnight. Where was he? The room seemed to be spinning around her, wrapping her up in its dark cocoon. She rocked back and forth, clutching Gordon's still warm body to her chest, moaning softly at the growing realization that she had been set up—they both had. Jeremy must have sent Gordon the same coordinates and time he had texted her. He had pitted them against each other, fully intending for one of them to die here tonight.

"Call for backup," Mallory yelled to Hal as he and Brent sprinted from the sheriff station and jumped into their cruiser shortly after midnight. Brent took the wheel and, seconds later, they peeled out of the parking lot, siren blaring and lights flashing.

Mallory tightened his bulletproof vest as he went over in his mind what had transpired. The 911 call had come from remote coordinates close to an abandoned hunting cabin. The police dispatcher who took the call recognized Tammy's voice, noting that she was under duress. She had lost connection before the dispatcher could make much sense of what she was saying other than that she needed an ambulance right away. The dispatcher thought he heard her mumble something that sounded like Galbraith, but Mallory didn't know if that meant Melanie or Gordon.

Blood pounded in his veins as he and Brent sped toward the forest. What was Tammy doing out here in the middle of the night anyway? She'd texted him earlier to say she was spending the night with friends. Was she in trouble? Had Gordon abducted her or hurt her? Threatened to kill her? He must be aware of the role she'd played in Melanie's disappearance. Patricia would have told him everything by now. He might be holding Tammy hostage until Melanie was returned safely. And where was Melanie in all of this? Mallory gritted his teeth as they drove, praying the ambulance that was being dispatched wasn't for the kid. If Tammy had hurt that little girl, he would be hard pressed to keep from laying into her himself.

The roads were deserted at this time of night and they soon reached a turnoff to the forest service road the GPS was directing them to turn down. They followed it for another two miles to a trailhead. Seconds later, Mallory spotted the glint of metal through the trees. "Hold up! There's a vehicle down there by the river!"

Brent swung the steering wheel hard left and bumped over the root-ridden dirt track down to a deserted campsite.

Mallory shone a search light over the license plate of a black Cadillac and pulled out his notebook to double check the number. "It's Gordon Galbraith's. Let's check it out." He opened the glove box in the police cruiser and removed a small spring-loaded tool for breaking glass.

Brent shoved the squad car into park, unholstered his weapon and climbed out, sweeping the area with a circumspect gaze. He padded toward the driver's side of Gordon's Cadillac, gun drawn, while Mallory approached from the passenger's side, and shone a light around the interior. He tried the door handle but the car was locked.

"There's a suitcase inside, sir," Brent observed.

Mallory's stomach churned with dread as he studied it. It was just about big enough to hide a small child in. He quickly lined up the tool in his hand and smashed the window before wrenching open the door. With a quick steadying breath, he unzipped the suitcase, praying his worst fears would prove to be unfounded. He flipped open the lid and exhaled in silent relief at the sight of the empty interior. He dug around in the foam base lining the case with his fingers and pulled out a small canister of silica gel, holding it up for Brent to see. "I'm willing to bet Gordon doesn't need this to keep his clothes dry. There was a weapon in here, maybe more than one."

"Clever," Brent commented. "A gun case disguised as a suitcase. A professional touch."

"Radio the location in and have his car impounded," Mallory replied. "We need to keep moving toward the coordinates. If Melanie's here, she must be up at the cabin."

He took a few quick pictures of the vehicle before joining Brent back in the police cruiser. "Turn off the lights. I don't want to be a sitting duck if this turns into a shootout."

Brent obliged, then backed up the vehicle and pulled out onto the forest service road again.

Moments later, Mallory leaned forward and pointed at a trail marker up ahead. "That's us. The hunting cabin is somewhere on this hillside."

Brent parked the squad car off to the side of the road and cut the engine.

"Sure you're ready to do this, boss?" he asked, his brow rumpled in concern. "The dispatcher seemed pretty sure that was Tammy's voice he heard. We can wait for backup if you want."

Mallory clenched his jaw. "We're the first officers on the scene. We're going in." He checked to make sure his weapon was loaded, then turned on his flashlight and climbed out of the car.

They ascended the trail in silence, the steep elevation taxing their lungs as they strove to keep up a steady pace. Dense undergrowth encroached on their path, and every so often, the skittering sound of a foraging rodent made them flinch and tighten their grip on their weapons. Determination drove Mallory's legs forward. Despite the heavy weight in his chest, he refused to let himself dwell on what he might find at the cabin, reminding himself that this was about an innocent child who had become a pawn to everyone around her. Tammy's safety was at best a secondary consideration.

After a quarter mile or so, the trail leveled out and Brent and Mallory took a minute to catch their breath before proceeding. They stepped carefully around and over any dry branches liable to snap beneath their feet and alert anyone lurking in the vicinity to their presence. When the outline of the hunting cabin came into view, Mallory switched off his flashlight and motioned to Brent to follow him. A cold sweat prickled on the back of his neck and, despite his resolve, a shiver ran through him. Had they come too late to save Melanie?

"You all right, boss?" Brent whispered.

Mallory gave a grim nod. "Let's do this."

As they padded forward, the faint wail of an ambulance carried through the air. They approached the dilapidated wooden structure from either side, weapons drawn, closing in on twenty feet. Mallory kept his breathing slow and even. Still no sign of movement.

"Police! Come out with your hands raised!" he yelled.

Seconds ticked by, punctuated only by a pair of birds fluttering out of a nearby tree. No one responded to Mallory's command, and no one appeared in the half-open door of the cabin.

Mallory grimaced, willing Tammy to have the sense to comply if she was inside. "Tammy, if you can hear me, answer me, or come on out now. It's over."

He turned to Brent. "Cover me, I'm going in."

He crept stealthily toward the wooden structure, swathed in gloom. As he approached, his eyes made out a prostrate body just inside the doorway. "Man down!" he called back to Brent as he shone his flashlight over the man's face. "Watch our perimeter in case the killer's still out there." Grimacing, Mallory took a knee and checked for a pulse, confirming that Gordon Galbraith was dead. He immediately turned his attention to the rest of the room, noting the black bag in the middle of the table. Some kind of deal had gone down in here and it had gone horribly wrong for Gordon. Mallory's eyes swept the room again. There was no sign of Tammy or Melanie. Had they come and gone already? A gurgling sound to his left made the hairs on the back of his neck stand on end. He stepped over Gordon's body, then cautiously side-stepped around the door, weapon raised. Bile rose up from his stomach at the sight of the familiar figure slumped against the cabin wall, long black strands of hair matted across her bloodied face.

Mallory holstered his gun and dropped to his knees at his wife's side. "Tammy! Tammy, can you hear me?" His voice cracked as he took her in his arms. Her eyes were closed and her breathing shallow. He quickly assessed her condition. There was a gunshot wound to her right temple. He groaned when he spotted the gun lying on the floor just out of reach of her blood-red nails. "Why, Tammy? Why?" he screamed in frustration. "Was he worth it?"

Anger and grief merged in a sea of emotion as he thought about what she had done—to herself, to him, to Melanie and her family. For a fleeting moment, his hand hovered over Tammy's face as he imagined covering her mouth and nose and finishing what she had started. No one would be any the wiser. Some might even consider it a merciful act. But he knew his conscience would never let him forget what he had done, and then she would haunt him forever. He hastily yanked his hand back from her face. He wasn't that kind of man, and he wouldn't let her make him become that kind of man, even now.

A radio crackled and Mallory shivered at the sudden touch of Brent's hand on his shoulder.

"Perimeter's clear. Is she alive, boss?"

"She's breathing, barely," Mallory replied, his voice raspy with emotion.

"Don't give up! The paramedics are coming up the trail," Brent assured him. "Backup's here."

Mallory gave a weary nod. "Have them search the surrounding area for any sign of Jeremy Ward. If he had a hand in setting up this rendezvous, he might just be sick enough to hang around and watch it play out."

Brent disappeared back outside again and, a moment later, voices drifted toward the cabin. Mallory wiped a hand across his brow. The paramedics would arrive at any minute. Tammy had one last chance to redeem herself.

"Tammy, listen to me, this is important. Do you know where Melanie is?" Mallory's voice shook as he stared down at the ghostly pallor of his wife as she struggled to take a rattling breath. Was she too far gone to answer the question? Did she even know the answer? "You'll ... " Tammy began in a hoarse whisper so faint that Mallory had to lean his ear close to her lips to hear her. "You'll never ... find ... her."

The blood in Mallory's veins ran cold. Part of him wanted to strangle the information out of her. But, he needed to try and keep her alive, not for his sake, but in case she knew something about Melanie's whereabouts. "Ssh, don't try and talk anymore," he soothed, holding her to his chest until the pounding of footsteps drew closer.

Two paramedics glided through the door carrying a stretcher, hesitating when they caught sight of Mallory cradling his wife.

Brent brushed past the paramedics. "Come on, boss," he urged, locking eyes with Mallory. "Give her up. They'll take good care of her."

After the paramedics had eased Tammy from his arms and strapped her to the stretcher, Mallory got to his feet in a trance. He watched the blur of activity as forensics lit the place up and began reconstructing the crime scene. Brent and another officer silently zipped Gordon into a body bag while the paramedics worked to stabilize Tammy. Mallory exited the cabin and left them to it. He didn't need anyone to tell him what he already knew. Tammy had killed Gordon and then tried to kill herself. The only question now was where were Jeremy and Melanie?

33

*M*allory stood on the rickety porch outside the hunting cabin watching the activity as officers combed through the surrounding brush looking for evidence or any sign of Jeremy Ward.

Moments later, Brent joined him and laid a gentle hand on his shoulder. "I'm so sorry, boss. Tammy didn't make it."

Mallory swallowed the jagged lump in his throat, his scrambled thoughts playing havoc with his warring emotions. He stood in silence as the paramedics carried her out, her blood soaking through the sheet covering her head.

"I can take over from here," Brent said. "You should go to the hospital with her."

Mallory locked eyes with him and shook his head. "Not for a DOA when that little four-year-old girl Tammy abducted is still missing."

Shock flickered across Brent's face. It didn't faze Mallory in the least. His relationship with Tammy had died a long time ago and whether or not he was by her side now wouldn't bring her back, but there was still a chance he could save Melanie. He'd promised Ava he'd do everything in his power to find her daughter and he fully intended to keep that promise. He turned and walked back inside the cabin to examine the crime scene more closely. Forensics was already at work taking blood samples and marking out the trajectory of the shots fired and the position of the bodies.

"See that, boss?" Brent pointed to the far corner of the room. "Looks like someone's been hiding out here."

Mallory walked over to inspect a deflated air mattress. He grimaced. Jeremy Ward had likely used the air compressor at his parents' place to blow it up. But, had he been holding Melanie here in the cabin? And, if so, where had he taken her? "Let's leave this to forensics," Mallory said. "We need to inform Ava Galbraith of what's happened, and then turn up the heat on the manhunt for Jeremy Ward before he gets too far."

A LITTLE AFTER three in the morning, Mallory and Brent pulled up outside Ava's cabin and hammered on the front door, leaving the cruiser lights flashing. "Police! Open up!"

After a few minutes of stomping their feet and rubbing their hands together to keep warm, Ava Galbraith pulled the door open a fraction and peered around it. Her eyes darted from Brent to Mallory, but not in the manner of a mother fearing dire news of her missing daughter. A flicker of curiosity at best.

"Can we come in?' Mallory asked in a somber tone. "It's about Gordon."

Ava's expression didn't change as she gestured them inside and tightened her robe around her. In the background, the low tones of the television murmured indicating that she hadn't gone to bed yet, or perhaps that she'd dozed off on the couch. She led them over to the rustic kitchen table and invited them to sit. "Do you want some coffee?" she offered.

"No, thank you." Mallory pulled off his hat and set it on his lap. "Ava, I'm sorry to have to inform you that your husband has been shot and killed."

She pressed her palm against her cheek and let out a ragged breath. "Poor Melanie, poor little lamb," she whispered, more to herself than anyone else. After a moment, she gave a dry-eyed nod. "I'm not surprised. It was a dangerous game he was playing."

Mallory hesitated, thrown off by her comment. "What game are you referring to?"

She dropped her gaze and picked at her fingers. "I've been aware of my husband's illicit activities for the best part of a year now, both in the boardroom and in the bedroom. I always thought a deal gone wrong would take him in the end."

Mallory shifted on his seat uncomfortably. "By illicit bedroom activities, I take it you're referring to his affair with Tammy?"

Ava shot him a look of sympathy. "I didn't have the heart to tell you. She's one of many."

"Was," Mallory corrected her. "She killed Gordon and then shot herself."

Ava's lips parted. Her eyes steered in Brent's direction as if seeking confirmation. "I'm ... so terribly sorry."

Mallory shook his head. "Don't be on my account. It's a shock, naturally, but our marriage died a long time ago."

Ava's eyes glistened. "I can relate to that."

Brent cleared his throat. "What can you tell us about your husband's illicit business ventures?"

"He was money laundering for a network of drug dealers and sex traffickers," Ava said with a sigh. "Jeremy Ward was part of his inner circle before he got busted and sent to prison. When I found out what Gordon was involved in, it was the final straw for me in terms of our marriage. I knew he didn't love me—I could live with that. But he was putting Melanie's life at risk and I couldn't stand by and allow that to happen any longer. He threatened to kill me when I asked for a divorce, and I knew he meant it. His contacts were dangerous people. I had to come up with a different plan to get away from him. I didn't have any money of my own so I took out a loan against the cabin."

"Are you willing to come down to the station and give us a statement?" Mallory asked.

"I am now that Melanie and I are safe."

Mallory's brows shot up. For a moment he thought he'd misunderstood, but the startled look on Brent's face told him he'd heard the same thing. "What do you mean? Do you know where Melanie is?"

"She's with my Aunt Delia in Cedarville." Ava let out a shuddering sigh. "It's a long story, but I had to go along with the kidnapping of my own daughter to ensure her safety."

Mallory exchanged another bewildered look with Brent and then frowned. "Are you saying you staged the abduction from Patricia's house?"

"Not exactly." Ava wiped her ragged fingertip across the table and then looked directly at Mallory. "Your wife planned that. She persuaded Patricia to take Melanie to her house to teach me a lesson. Unbeknownst to Patricia, Tammy had secretly hired Jeremy Ward to abduct Melanie from her grandmother's house and dispose of her."

"That's a serious allegation," Brent interjected.

"Yes it is," Ava replied firmly. "Which is why I made sure I obtained evidence to back it up. Jeremy Ward recorded his phone conversations with Tammy."

Mallory smoothed a shaking hand over his hair. It was one thing knowing that his wife had schemed to punish Gordon and frighten Ava by abducting Melanie, but to go so far as to plan to do away with an innocent child was even more sick and twisted than he had ever imagined her to be. Had he actually been living with a human being capable of such a thing? Granted, Tammy had deceived him by carrying on with Gordon all these years—evidently he had never really known the woman he'd been married to at all.

"So why did you go along with this kidnapping if you knew what Tammy and Jeremy intended to do to Melanie?" Brent asked.

"Jeremy had no stomach to kill a child," Ava replied. "When Tammy propositioned him, he called me and told me everything. It was a simple case of loyalty on his part. I hired Jeremy for a different job long before Tammy approached him. Together, we came up with a plan to get Melanie to safety and expose Tammy in the process."

"How did you know Jeremy Ward?" Mallory asked.

"I bumped into him when I was doing a photo shoot in the backcountry last spring. He was setting up his game camera." Ava gave a wry grin. "I guess you could say we connected over our cameras—we both shared a love of photography and wildlife. Eventually, he told me the whole story about how Gordon framed him for a heist gone bad years ago, then threatened his parents' lives if he ever ratted him out. Jeremy used to come back and visit his parents on the QT every so often. They were sworn to secrecy of course which was why Walt lied about that when you asked him."

"What did you hire Jeremy for?" Mallory prodded.

"I asked him to set up several game cameras on the cabin. They were well-camouflaged—Jeremy was a pro at that kind of thing. I'd long suspected Gordon was coming up here on weekends when he said he was attending conferences or traveling for business. I needed evidence of his criminal connections." A solitary tear tracked down her cheek. "I was going to use the evidence to blackmail Gordon into giving me sole custody. I knew he wouldn't want to go to court and face having his business ventures investigated."

"Go on," Mallory encouraged her gently.

"The cameras documented Gordon meeting armed men in the middle of the night and accepting deliveries. One weekend when Gordon was off playing golf, I searched the garage and found a false panel in the drywall. Once I realized the ceiling in our garage was full of money and weapons, I knew I had to leave him as soon as possible. It was too dangerous for Melanie to be around him anymore. It was only a matter of time before he ran afoul of the law, or a hitman." She hesitated and twisted her hands in her lap. "The game cameras also made it clear that he and Tammy were an item. But I'd already figured that out."

Ava placed her phone on the table between them. "The evidence is all here. Also, the details of the deal I made with Jeremy. He took Melanie from Patricia's house straight to my Aunt Delia. He snowmobiled over the mountains and met her as a designated spot to avoid the road block."

"What about the ransom demand? Where does that come into play?" Mallory asked.

"That was an addendum from Jeremy," Ava said with an apologetic shrug. "He figured Gordon owed him enough for a fresh start."

"Is he willing to make a statement to back up your story?" Mallory pressed.

Ava arched a regretful brow at him. "You'll have a hard time tracking him down. He has more than enough now to make him comfortable wherever he decides to live off-grid, in Alaska or south of the border. He seemed pretty determined to disappear for good this time, and if you want my opinion, you should let him. He saved my daughter's life by thwarting Tammy's plan." Ava stared at Mallory for a long uncomfortable moment. "If your wife had had her way, I would be planning Melanie's funeral right about now."

34

*A*va hummed along with Melanie as they wound their way toward the Oregon coast where Ava had rented the perfect beach cottage for a mother-daughter weekend. This time it really would be the official start of a new chapter. In the past few weeks, she had closed down her Instagram account and launched her photography business website. She no longer felt under pressure to take an endless stream of photos everywhere she went to satisfy the voracious appetites of her social media followers. She could give Melanie her undivided attention when she was with her, and when she was at work photographing events she would dedicate one-hundred-percent to her job. She had learned the hard way that there wasn't a good way to multi-task when it came to her daughter's safety.

The ransom money she had squirreled away was more than adequate to fund their new life until her business took off. Aunt Delia had met her the night of the "drop that wasn't" and taken the money to her place in Cedarville. The ransom hadn't been part of Ava's original plan, but once she'd realized it would trigger the FBI's involvement, she'd recognized it would be the safest way to expose Gordon's illegal business ventures while gaining custody of Melanie. Ava had a feeling Mallory knew that Jeremy Ward hadn't absconded with the ransom money—at least not all of it—but he hadn't pursued the matter. She knew he felt a huge burden of guilt for his wife's role in Melanie's abduction, and as a result he'd turned a blind eye to the things that didn't quite add up about the case. After all, it was Tammy who had set the whole thing in motion, and Tammy who had ordered a hit on Melanie. Mallory must have been relieved in one sense that his wife had taken her own life in the end so he wasn't forced to testify against her and then watch her languish in prison for the remainder of her days.

Ava couldn't help but feel sorry for Mallory at Tammy's funeral. He'd been forced to play the part of a grieving husband while coming to terms with a betrayal that had spanned his entire marriage. He deserved better. He was a kind and loyal man who had been beguiled by Tammy's looks and taken in by her wiles. Gordon, on the other hand, had known exactly who Tammy was, a narcissist with an ego as big as his own, and that had been the attraction between them from the outset—a deadly one as it turned out. Egos like that couldn't survive in another's shadow. Ava didn't regret for one minute asking Jeremy to send Gordon the same coordinates that he had sent to Tammy. Ava had orchestrated the showdown knowing full well that both of them would go to the cabin armed and fully intending to put an end to Jeremy Ward. It seemed fitting that Tammy and Gordon had each headed to the rendezvous point with hate in their hearts and the intent to kill. Fate had given them what they wanted.

Ava had played her final scene to perfection as Gordon's grieving widow. She'd attended his funeral dressed in designer black but felt nothing other than relief to see his casket lowered into the ground. Now, her new life was finally about to begin. She wasn't sure yet exactly what it would entail, but she was leaving all the possibilities open. Mallory had asked her to call him and let him know how she was doing once she was settled somewhere. And perhaps she would one day, when she was ready. But, for now, her focus was on the daughter she'd almost lost forever.

"Mommy, look!" Melanie squealed from her carseat. "It's the beach! Can I dig now, *please?*"

Ava smiled to herself as she glanced in the rearview mirror. "Why not? Let's do it." She pulled off the coastal highway at the next exit, rolling down the windows as they drove toward the crashing waves along the pristine stretch of sand stretched out in front of them. She was eager to get to their rental cottage and relax with a glass of wine after the long drive, but she was also more than willing to learn from her young daughter how to be spontaneous again, something she had forgotten how to do under Gordon's overbearing tutelage. Before she'd left the cabin at Brooksbury, she'd written down all her fears and then read the list out loud before burning it in the fireplace. A symbolic final act of rebellion as she broke free from her past. From now on, she would live life with abandon. There was nothing to run from anymore, no need to look over her shoulder.

Despite Patricia's protestations, the family cabin was up for sale, marking the end of an era and the beginning of a new one for everyone involved. The proceeds would be used to pay back the loan she had taken out against it. She had hidden a good portion of that money in the deep freezer in the cabin with the intention of using it in her bid for freedom. The FBI had seized it, believing it to be drug money, and Ava hadn't corrected them. She'd been thankful enough not to be prosecuted for forgery. Besides, she had four-hundred-and-fifty-thousand dollars to start a new life with now.

She had turned over the game camera Jeremy left for her in Walt's workshop to Mallory. It contained all the footage he needed to go after several prominent businessmen running sex trafficking rings and drug smuggling operations— Gordon's seedy associates. The game camera also contained a fair amount of footage of Gordon and Tammy entering the cabin together, fawning all over each other. Ava hoped Mallory had the sense not to bother viewing it.

Melanie pointed excitedly through the open window to a flock of birds flying overhead, and a group of horses meandering along a nearby trail. Ava was grateful that to date her daughter showed no signs of trauma after everything she'd gone through. Thanks to the sleeping medication in the hot chocolate Patrica had given her, she'd woken up at Aunt Delia's place in Cedarville and never known that a man called Jeremy Ward had taken her from her grandmother's house, and driven her through the backcountry on a snowmobile to a meeting point south of Brooksbury. Maybe it was for the best if she never heard the story.

When Ava reached the beach parking lot, she turned off the engine and helped Melanie out of her booster seat. Together they rummaged among their luggage in the back until they found Melanie's new bucket and spade that they'd purchased especially for this trip. Taking her daughter by the hand, Ava led her over the dunes, smiling at a young couple as they went by, arms entwined around each other's waists. It had been a month since Gordon's death, and the heaviness that Ava had lived with for so many years had lifted at last. She was free of the Galbraiths, even Gordon's insufferable mother. As a result of Patricia's role in Melanie's abduction, she'd been denied visitation rights by the judge at the custody hearing.

Melanie tugged on Ava's hand and looked up at her. "Can we run, Mommy?"

Ava nodded, blinking back tears of relief and joy and thankfulness. She was especially grateful to Jeremy Ward for everything he had done to help her. She wished him well wherever he ended up. Like him, she had been given a second chance, but it was only by finding the resolve within herself that she had been able to avail of it. It had been hard to stay strong when she was used to being weak, and it had been particularly difficult to hold the course when Melanie was taken from her. She'd finally forgiven herself for her mistakes and no longer replayed that fateful morning in her head, choosing instead to live each moment intentionally and find the good in her journey. She laughed along with Melanie as they tripped through the sand, the salty tang of the air on her tongue a welcome reminder that they had lived to see the dawn of this new day.

"Race you!" she said, smiling down at her daughter as she released her grip and let go of Melanie's tiny hand. She inhaled a deep breath of ocean air. This time everything would be all right. She could let go without fear of what might happen. Melanie would come back to her because Ava would be right there by her side to make sure of it.

THE OTHER WOMAN

Ready for another suspense-filled read with shocking plot twists and turns along the way? Check out my psychological thriller *The Other Woman* on Amazon!

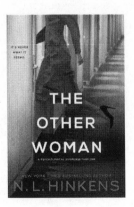

Not all secrets are what they seem.
When Bridget spots an elegantly dressed woman leaving her husband's office late one night, she fears the worst. Her marriage is already strained but things are about to take an even more shocking turn when her family is suddenly torn

apart by a horrific crime they all become entangled in. Her trust is shattered, her husband is on the run, and her son is hiding a dark secret. Bridget's life has become a dangerous lie and the clock is ticking as the police close in on the killer.

Who can she trust, when all roads lead back to her husband and son?

- A gripping thriller that will leave you doubting those you love most! -

Do you enjoy reading across genres? I also write young adult science fiction and fantasy thrillers. You can find out more about those titles at **www.normahinkens.com.**

A QUICK FAVOR

Dear Reader,

I hope you enjoyed reading *Her Last Steps* as much as I enjoyed writing it. Thank you for taking the time to check out my books and I would appreciate it from the bottom of my heart if you would leave a review, long or short, on Amazon as it makes a HUGE difference in helping new readers find the series. Thank you!

To be the first to hear about my upcoming book releases, sales, and fun giveaways, sign up for my newsletter at **www.normahinkens.com** and follow me on Twitter, Instagram and Facebook. Feel free to email me at norma@normahinkens.com with any feedback or comments. I LOVE hearing from readers. YOU are the reason I keep going through the tough times.

All my best,
Norma

BIOGRAPHY

NYT and USA Today bestselling author Norma Hinkens writes twisty psychological suspense thrillers, as well as fast-paced science fiction and fantasy about spunky heroines and epic adventures in dangerous worlds. She's also a travel junkie, legend lover, and idea wrangler, in no particular order. She grew up in Ireland, land of make-believe and the original little green man.

Find out more about her books on her website.
www.normahinkens.com

Follow her on Facebook for funnies, giveaways, cool stuff & more!

Made in the USA
Columbia, SC
20 January 2022

54547125R00145

BOOKS BY NORMA HINKENS

I also write young adult science fiction and fantasy thrillers under Norma Hinkens.

www.normahinkens.com/books

THE UNDERGROUNDERS SERIES - POST-APOCALYPTIC
Immurement
Embattlement
Judgement

THE EXPULSION PROJECT - SCIENCE FICTION
Girl of Fire
Girl of Stone
Girl of Blood

THE KEEPERS CHRONICLES - EPIC FANTASY
Opal of Light
Onyx of Darkness
Opus of Doom

Follow Norma:

Sign up for her newsletter:

https://books.normahinkens.com/VIPReaderClub

Website:

https://normahinkens.com/

Facebook:

https://www.facebook.com/NormaHinkensAuthor/

Twitter

https://twitter.com/NormaHinkens

Instagram

https://www.instagram.com/normahinkensauthor/

Pinterest:

https://www.pinterest.com/normahinkens/

Made in the USA
Columbia, SC
20 January 2022